SCENT OF FEAR

A CHRISTIAN ROMANTIC SUSPENSE

SULLIVAN K9 SEARCH AND RESCUE

LAURA SCOTT

1

———

Libby Tolliver shifted the bag of groceries in her arms so she could open the door to her grandfather's cabin. "Grandpa? It's Libby."

Her sixty-nine-year-old grandfather wasn't in the kitchen or living room from what she could see. She frowned as she strode to the kitchen to drop the bag of groceries on the counter. "Grandpa?" Her grandfather was usually up and about by now, despite his arthritic hips. She turned and headed down the hallway to the two bedrooms. Her grandfather, Marvin Tolliver, wasn't in the main bedroom, the guest room she used when she came to visit, or the bathroom.

An icy finger of fear snaked down her spine. Her grandpa wasn't prone to wandering around, but maybe something outside had caught his attention? As it was early June in Wyoming, the weather was mild. She swung open the patio door, then abruptly stopped.

One of two patio chairs was overturned, and there was a broken ceramic mug lying on the ground with a dark stain of what appeared to be spilled coffee. Her heart jumped in her throat as she frantically scanned the backyard.

"Grandpa!" she shouted at the top of her lungs. "Grandpa, it's Libby! Are you okay?"

She didn't see or hear anything. Libby pulled her phone from her pocket and called the Sullivan K9 Search and Rescue Ranch. She'd known Shane Sullivan in high school; he was a year ahead of her. Libby and Shane had never dated. Shane had been seeing a girl named Rebecca Yost, and there had been rumors of a possible engagement. Then Rebecca had died in a terrible car crash, and Shane had taken the loss hard. Especially since it was only a few years later that he'd lost his parents too.

Still, she knew Shane and the rest of his siblings had turned their parents' former glamorous dude ranch into a large K9 search and rescue operation. Libby held herself together with an effort as she waited for the call to go through.

"This is Anna. You've reached the Sullivan K9 Search and Rescue Ranch," a pleasant voice said.

"My name is Libby Tolliver. I'm looking for Shane. We went to high school together. My grandfather Marvin Tolliver is missing. He . . ." Her voice faltered for a moment. "It looks like he may have left under duress. Or ran into the woods because he was scared." That didn't sound like her tough-as-nails grandfather, but she couldn't imagine another scenario. "All I know for sure is that he's missing, and I need someone to come search for him."

"I'll send Shane and his K9, Bryce, right away," Anna assured her. "What's the address?"

"My grandfather lives a few miles east of Greybull," Libby said, and provided the exact address. "How long will it take for Shane to get here?"

"I'm not sure, but he'll get to your location as soon as possible."

"Okay, thank you." She ended the call, then headed back into the kitchen to put the perishable items she'd purchased in the fridge and freezer before heading back outside to the patio. It occurred to her that she should notify the police.

As she pulled out her phone to make the call, it rang. She quickly answered. "Hello?"

"Libby? It's Shane. I'm halfway between Cody and Greybull and should be there soon. What happened?" Shane's gruff voice helped soothe her nerves.

"I don't know exactly." She stared off at the woods that stretched toward the mountains. "I grocery shop for my grandfather on Saturdays, but he wasn't here when I arrived. One of the patio chairs is lying on its side, and his coffee mug is broken on the concrete." She tried to maintain a positive attitude. "Maybe he saw something amazing and rushed out to get a closer look at it."

"Really?" Shane's voice was thick with doubt.

She tried not to sigh. "I don't know, but I'll head out to start searching. My grandfather has an arthritic hip, so I'm worried he may have fallen. Just get here soon, okay?"

"I will, but don't head out yet. Wait for me. Oh, and gather some of your grandfather's recently worn clothing together. Bryce will use them as a scent source."

"I can do that." Libby normally did her grandfather's laundry on Saturdays, too, so she knew there would be a full hamper to choose from. She didn't like the idea of waiting, but it helped to know he was closer than she'd expected. "Thanks, Shane."

"I'll be there ASAP." He ended the call without saying anything more.

Libby hurried down the hall to her grandpa's room and

hauled the hamper of dirty clothes into the living room. Then she headed back outside, giving the patio a wide berth to head toward the woods.

"Grandpa? Grandpa, it's Libby! Can you hear me?" Hearing nothing, she fought to remain calm. If her grandfather had fallen, he might have hit his head and lost consciousness. "Grandpa! We're coming to find you! Don't worry, we'll find you!"

Still no response. Sweeping her gaze over the area, she tried to figure out which path her grandfather had taken. It was a foolish attempt on her part because she had no experience with hunting or tracking. The smart thing to do would be to wait for Shane and his dog.

Yet she didn't immediately turn back toward the cabin. Realizing she still hadn't called the police, she pulled her phone out again.

But after staring at the screen for a long moment, she tucked the device back into her pocket. Maybe it was better to wait. A tipped-over chair and broken mug didn't really indicate a crime had taken place. Especially way out here in the middle of nowhere. The more she considered that, the less likely she believed he'd been taken away by force. Maybe her grandfather had been startled by something, maybe a bear or some other wild animal, jumped to his feet, and then . . . went to see the animal up close?

She winced. Maybe not. Her grandfather could have simply wandered off. He could have fallen off his chair, broken his cup, and gotten angry with himself, so he'd gone into the woods. Or he'd been confused. She'd noticed his memory wasn't what it used to be.

"Grandpa? Can you hear me?"

The silence was deafening. Libby ran her fingers

through her reddish hair and reluctantly turned to head back to the cabin.

After what seemed like forever, she heard the rumble of an approaching car. She hurried out front, watching as a black SUV bounced up the driveway. Shane stopped behind her red pickup truck and slid out from behind the wheel. He was tall and lean, with dark-brown hair and mesmerizing blue eyes. He gave her a nod as the back hatch sprung open, and a huge German shepherd bounded out. Libby took a hasty step backward, fearing the dog would charge toward her.

"Bryce, heel," Shane commanded.

The dog whirled and went straight to Shane's side. The large black and tan dog sat and stared up at him expectantly.

"Good boy," Shane murmured. He raised his gaze to her. "Come closer, Libby. I want Bryce to know you're a friend."

Swallowing against a knot of fear, she crossed over to join them. Shane reached out for her hand, then brought it toward his dog's snout. "Friend, Bryce. Libby is a friend."

Bryce sniffed her fingers with interest, then gazed at her with his dark-brown eyes. His tail swished over the ground, but up close, the dog was still intimidating. She offered a weak smile. "Good doggy. No biting, okay?"

"Bryce won't bite you." Shane frowned. "Don't tell me you're afraid of dogs?"

"Okay, I won't tell you." She tugged her hand free and stepped back. "Not afraid exactly, just wary. I was bitten by a dog as a kid."

"I'm sorry to hear that, but I promise you don't have to be afraid of Bryce. He won't bite except on my command." As she was wondering how often he'd commanded his dog to bite,

Shane turned to head toward the rear hatch of his vehicle. "Let me get Bryce ready and we'll start the search. Do you have your grandfather's clothes?" At her nod, he continued. "If you could place a few items in a plastic bag, that would be good. Dirty socks work well and so do recently worn T-shirts."

Grateful for something to do, she said, "I'll get them."

A few minutes later, she returned to find Bryce wearing a K9 vest strapped around his torso. Shane had a large backpack slung over his shoulders and was chattering with the dog, asking if he was ready to play the search game. Bryce stared up at Shane, his tail wagging with excitement.

"Here." She handed him the bag containing four pairs of her grandfather's dirty socks and a worn T-shirt, trying not to get too close to Bryce.

"Thanks. You mentioned arthritis?" Shane arched a brow. "Any other medical issues I need to know about?"

"He's been a little more forgetful than usual," she admitted. "But he's sixty-nine and will be seventy in November. I figure that's just part of getting older, right?"

"Maybe." Shane was noncommittal. "What's your grandfather's name?"

"Marvin."

"Okay, thanks." He filled a collapsible bowl with water and set it before Bryce. The dog lowered his head, took a few laps of water, then stared up at Shane again. "Good boy, are you ready to search? Here, this is Marvin." Shane opened the bag of clothes. Bryce eagerly buried his snout in the clothing. "Marvin, Bryce. Search! Search for Marvin!"

After one last sniff in the bag, Bryce lifted his nose to the air, then turned and trotted toward the cabin. Shane hurried after his dog. Libby picked up her pace, too, already encouraged by Shane's professional approach to the search.

She was confident Shane and Bryce would find her

grandfather. The Sullivans had an amazing reputation for success. Everyone in the area sang their praises. This would work. She refused to consider the alternative.

Hang on, Grandpa! We're coming!

SHANE WAS FAR TOO aware of Libby beside him. Doing his best to ignore her flowery scent, he gave his K9, Bryce, plenty of room to work. He hadn't seen Libby in years, but she looked the same as he remembered. Her auburn hair was wavy and loose, the ends touching her shoulders, and the sprinkling of freckles across her nose made her look as young as she had been back in high school.

She was cute in the girl-next-door kind of way.

Not that he was interested in anything other than finding her grandfather. Just because his oldest siblings were falling in love left and right didn't mean he was joining the club. The girl he'd loved had died years ago. He wasn't interested in trying again.

Pushing thoughts of Libby and Rebecca from his mind, he focused on the mission at hand. At sixty-nine, Marvin Tolliver wasn't that old, but having arthritis meant the guy could have fallen and was right now lying out in the woods, unconscious.

If so, Bryce would find him.

Bryce trotted around the rustic log cabin, not unlike the one Shane lived in on the Sullivan ranch, then abruptly stopped and sniffed intently along the patio near the over-turned chair. Shane wasn't surprised when Bryce sat and let out a sharp bark, staring at him.

"Good boy, Bryce." He had Bryce's yellow rubber ducky in his pocket but didn't bring out the reward just yet. This was only the beginning of their game, and he wouldn't reward his K9 until they were further along in the process. "Search! Search for Marvin!"

Bryce eagerly jumped back into the search, sniffing the concrete patio, then trotting out over the grassy lawn toward the woods.

As they followed, he glanced at Libby. "Any idea how long your grandfather has been gone?"

She bit her lip. "Not really. He usually gets up around seven in the morning and eats breakfast, then has his coffee. He sits on the patio when the weather is nice." She glanced at her watch. "It's ten thirty, which means he could have left the patio a few hours ago."

"When's the last time you spoke to him?"

"Last night. I told him I'd be out this morning as usual." She sighed. "I do his grocery shopping every Saturday and then stay long enough to visit while doing his laundry. Grandpa can take care of himself, but I like seeing him each week. I'd drive over more often if I didn't have to work in the hospital billing department Monday through Friday. I've tried to encourage him to move to Cody, but he won't." There was a slight pause, before she added, "After this, I'll have to insist he move in with me. He won't like it, but obviously, he can't stay way out here by himself any longer."

He understood her concern. His attention swung toward Bryce. His K9 was sniffing intently as he moved through the woods, indicating he was hot on the scent. Shane quickened his pace to keep up, unwilling to lose sight of his K9. He and Bryce had been through many searches together. They worked best as a team.

Libby hurried forward too.

"If you need to head back to the cabin, that's fine." He

glanced at Libby, then nodded at Bryce. "I'll call you when we find him."

"I'm sticking with you." She sounded a little breathless. "And I appreciate your positive attitude."

He hid a grimace. He wasn't a positive-attitude kind of guy. His sisters teased him for his doom-and-gloom approach to life, and he couldn't deny his tendency to expect the worst. But he didn't want to worry Libby any more than she already was. Deep down, he suspected that her grandfather was probably hurt in some way; otherwise, he'd have come back to the cabin under his own power.

At this point, the best Shane could hope for was that they found Marvin alive.

Not dead.

He glanced at his watch. During the summer months, they made sure to take frequent water breaks to prevent the dogs from becoming dehydrated. Shane decided they'd walk for twenty minutes before stopping to rest.

"How do you know Bryce is following my grandfather's scent?" Libby asked. "I mean, he just seems to be randomly trotting through the brush."

"Bryce is a good tracker." He had confidence in his dog's ability. "If he lost the trail, he'd stop moving forward, turn around, and come back to the last point he'd located the scent."

"Okay, that helps." Libby's smile was sad. "I pray we find him soon."

Shane nodded, then narrowed his gaze as Bryce abruptly stopped near a fallen tree. His K9 sniffed intently around the log, then sat and let out a sharp bark. Bryce held Shane's gaze as if to say *I found him.*

"Is that an alert?" Libby asked, as Shane hurried over to his dog.

Shane scanned the ground beneath the fallen tree. The dry dirt didn't reveal any footprints, but Bryce had alerted there for a reason.

Had Marvin stopped there to rest? Or had he tripped and fallen? Maybe the old man was confused and managed to get up and continue his wandering path through the woods.

Then his gaze spotted a fuzzy red thread clinging to a spike branch of the fallen log. He glanced at Libby. "Do you have any idea what your grandfather is wearing?"

She looked confused. "Jeans, hiking boots, and a plaid shirt most likely, along with a cowboy hat. Why?"

"What color would his plaid shirt be?" Remembering she hadn't seen him this morning, he added, "Maybe a favorite color?"

"He has plaid shirts in just about every color—blue, green, red, and brown." She frowned. "Not black, though. And no light gray either."

The red thread could have been left by anyone at any time, yet Shane trusted Bryce's alert. "There's a red thread here."

Libby came up to stand beside him. Then she nodded slowly. "I don't remember seeing the red plaid shirt in his laundry basket, so he could be wearing it."

He nodded, then turned his attention to Bryce. "Good boy!" He pulled the yellow ducky from his pocket and tossed it into the air. "Good boy!"

Bryce ran after the ducky with excitement. He shook his head from side to side as he galloped through the brush. Watching his K9 play with his reward usually made Shane smile.

But he couldn't quite get rid of the niggling sense of concern. The overturned chair and the broken coffee mug indicated Marvin had been taken by surprise. And that surprise had—what? Caused him to take a walk in the woods?

Could Libby be right about something catching his attention enough to draw him away from the cabin and into the forest?

That theory didn't make sense. Libby's grandfather knew she was coming out to bring him groceries for the week. Marvin wouldn't just decide to take a day hike through the woods without waiting for her.

Unless the old man's memory was worse than Libby had indicated.

"Shane, I don't understand why you're playing with Bryce when we need to keep looking for my grandfather." She looked annoyed.

"I need to reward Bryce for the find; besides, it's time to give him more water." Since they'd already stopped there, Shane shrugged out of his backpack and set it on the ground. He filled the collapsible bowl with water. "Bryce, come."

The dog galloped toward him.

"Hand." Shane held out his hand for the yellow ducky. Bryce obediently regurgitated it into his palm, then lowered his head to lap at the water.

"Wow, that's amazing," Libby murmured, her previous annoyance having dissipated. "I can't believe he just hands over his toys."

"He's a good boy." Shane ruffled Bryce's fur. The dog's tail wagged as if in agreement. He held Bryce's gaze. "Sit." The shepherd lowered his back haunches. "Lie down." Now Bryce lowered the rest of his body so that he was stretched across the ground near the fallen log. "Good boy," he praised again.

Bryce understood this was a rest break. The Sullivan K9s were well trained and had done this often enough that they understood the routine. The only dog that tended to balk at orders was Chase's K9, Rocky.

Rocky's independent streak was a source of amusement for the rest of the siblings, mostly because Chase was the second oldest of the family and accustomed to being in charge. Rocky had a way of humbling their sometimes-bossy brother.

"I wish I understood why Grandpa came this way." Libby's voice interrupted his thoughts. "I wonder if he was following a wounded animal." Her eyes widened. "Maybe he saw a poacher and was determined to get proof to provide to the local game warden."

"Maybe." He figured that theory was slightly better than the idea the old man had decided to take a hike. "I haven't noticed any animal blood as we moved through the woods, though."

"I wasn't paying attention." She flushed. "I should have thought of that sooner."

"It doesn't matter, Bryce will follow your grandfather's scent, not that of a wounded animal." He stroked a hand over Bryce's fur. "Dogs can distinguish between two hundred million scents. Bryce will know a wild animal is nearby, but he'll stay focused on the search command I've given him."

"Wow." Libby looked at the dog with renewed respect. "That's amazing."

"Yeah." He emptied the water from the collapsible dish and tucked it away. "Ready, Bryce? Search! Search for Marvin!"

Bryce jumped to his feet without hesitation. The K9

sniffed near the fallen log, then began following the scent trail heading in a northeastern direction.

"How much land does your grandfather own?" He scanned the wilderness around them. "I'm just wondering if we'll end up trespassing on someone else's property."

"Grandpa owns about ten acres. The rest is public land. The Bighorn national park is a few miles from here too. That's federal land." She frowned. "It's all a little confusing to me. I guess everyone is supposed to know where the boundaries are located. Grandpa has complained about hunters being on his property, though."

"He's had trouble with the locals trespassing and hunting on his land?" He was intrigued by the idea of a poacher or two drawing her grandfather into the woods. Most hunters went out in pairs because an elk was too big for one man to haul out on his own.

Not that June was hunting season for elk or other big game.

"Not recently." Libby shrugged. "The last time he mentioned it was maybe two years ago. And I still think the hunters probably crossed the property line by mistake. Grandpa hasn't put up no hunting signs warning them away, so there's no way they could know they were trespassing."

"Yeah, but hunters are supposed to know where they can and can't hunt. Maybe he did hear a pair of poachers. A gunshot could have startled him enough to drop his coffee." Shane quickened his pace as Bryce followed the scent trail. "Maybe he jumped up, kicking the chair over to yell at them."

"That could be, but where is he now?" Libby's wide brown eyes were filled with concern. "Grandpa would answer us if he could."

Shane nodded. "I'm sure he would."

They followed in Bryce's wake for the next ten minutes. They were heading deeper into the woods now, and that was starting to worry him. How far would Marvin go to nab a poacher? Especially if he had arthritis in his hip?

Bryce jumped over a downed tree. The dog liked to run and jump, which meant Shane had to do the same.

"Hurry," he urged Libby. "I don't want to lose him."

"Don't worry. I'm coming." She gamely climbed up and over the log. "Why doesn't your dog take a straight—" Her comment was cut off by the crack of gunfire.

"Down!" Shane grabbed Libby's hand and yanked her down. "Bryce!" His shout was strangled. "Bryce, come!"

His breath froze in his throat as he waited for his K9 to return. The gunfire may prove their theory about poachers drawing her grandfather into the woods, but why would a hunter shoot at them?

Shane had a bad feeling that there was more going on here than Libby's missing grandfather. And he didn't like knowing he, Libby, and Bryce were in danger.

2

Crouched beside Shane and partially hidden behind a tree, Libby's heart raced. What in the world was going on? She glanced around, trying to spot the poacher. It had to be the same person who'd drawn her grandfather into the woods.

"Bryce!" Shane's voice rose in agitation. Then the tan and black German shepherd bounded toward them. Shane put his arm around the dog's neck and pulled him close, relief etched on his features. "Good boy."

"Do you see the poacher?" She kept her voice low. "Can you tell where the shot came from?"

"It's hard to say for sure." Shane's expression turned grim. "But I don't like this. Whoever took that shot came close to hitting us."

She didn't like their tenuous situation either, but her grandfather was still missing, and they needed to find him. They huddled at the base of a tree for several long minutes until she thought she might scream. "We need to keep moving," she finally said.

"I'm not risking you or my dog." Shane scowled. "Better that we head back to the cabin and call the police."

"But Bryce was following my grandfather's scent!" Libby put a hand on Shane's arm. "Please, Shane, don't give up the search. What if Grandpa is hurt and waiting for us to find him?"

Shane's frown deepened. "I don't like this," he repeated, half under his breath. "I can't figure out if that shot was intended to kill us or was simply fired as a warning."

"A warning?" She didn't understand.

"Maybe the poacher is trying to force us to go back to the cabin." He pinned her with a somber gaze. "It could be his illegal carcass is strung up in a tree nearby, and he doesn't want us to see what he shot and killed."

"I don't care about illegal poaching!" She raised her voice loud enough that she hoped the shooter could hear. "Don't you understand? I only want to find my grandfather!"

There was nothing but a long silence after her outburst. She felt a little foolish talking to someone she couldn't see. Yet the gunshot had been very real.

Shane shook his head without saying anything. He also didn't appear in a hurry to move. She understood his desire to keep them safe, but they couldn't just sit out here forever.

Inactivity chafed as they remained in place for a full ten minutes before Shane slowly stood. He didn't look happy but glanced down at Bryce with a resigned expression. "Okay, we'll keep going for a while longer. But if this guy fires at us again, we're done."

"Thanks for agreeing to continue the search." She wasn't about to agree to being done. She had no intention of leaving the woods without her grandfather. "Grandpa needs us."

He sighed, then looked down at Bryce. "Are you ready to search? Search for Marvin!"

Bryce's tail wagged as the dog turned and headed back to the trail. Shane gestured for her to go next. She tipped her head, sending him a questioning look.

"I'll cover you from behind," he said gruffly. "Go. We need to keep up with Bryce."

It seemed useless to argue, so she hurried after the large dog. Watching Bryce follow her grandfather's scent trail was amazing and helped ease some of her wariness toward large breed dogs. Not that she intended to get too close to Bryce's sharp, ferocious teeth.

She quickened her pace, trying not to let the dog out of sight. She found herself hunching her shoulders, expecting more gunfire, but she only heard the rustling sounds they made moving through the woods. Maybe the poacher had moved on with his illegal game.

She would rather believe the guy had given up and left the area than consider the possibility that he was following them.

Libby concentrated on pushing ahead. She noticed that the path Bryce took had less foliage to push out of the way. And every so often, she saw a broken tree branch, giving credence to the theory that her grandpa had come this way.

They had to find him! A sense of urgency spurred her forward. When Bryce stopped at a boulder sitting off to the side of what appeared to be a worn path, sniffing the ground intently, she turned to look at Shane. "Shouldn't he bark if he's alerting?"

"Yes." The moment Shane answered, Bryce abruptly sat and let out a sharp bark.

Libby hurried forward. The boulder was about as high as her knee. Her grandpa was roughly six feet tall and carried a few extra pounds on his frame. It wasn't a stretch to imagine him sitting down on the boulder to rest.

She dropped down onto the rock, mirroring her grandfather's movements. Had he sat there for a few minutes, listening for the poacher? And if so, why had he kept pushing forward? Why not give up the search and head back to the cabin? Especially since he knew she'd be arriving with his groceries?

It didn't make sense, but Bryce had alerted there, so she believed her grandfather had stopped there at least for a few minutes.

"Good boy," Shane praised. He tossed the yellow rubber ducky high in the air. Bryce jumped up to catch it, then ran around with the prize in his mouth.

The dog's antics made her smile. "I thought you didn't want to reward him every time he alerted?"

"Normally, I wouldn't, but the crack of gunfire interrupted the game. Bryce is a good tracker. I need him to stay engaged in the search." Shane frowned. "I still don't like that someone took a shot at us. I hope we find your grandfather soon."

"Me too." She wanted nothing more than to get her grandfather back home where he belonged. "Bryce will find him."

"He will." Shane gave a curt nod, then glanced at his dog. Shane didn't smile often, but his expression softened when he addressed his partner. "Bryce, come!"

The large dog galloped over to Shane's side, the yellow ducky looking ridiculous in his clenched teeth.

"Hand." Bryce held out his hand expectantly. Bryce dropped the toy into Shane's outstretched palm. "Good boy." He bent and ruffled the dog's fur, then he shrugged out of his pack and poured some water into the collapsible bowl. Seeing the water made her realize how thirsty she was.

She'd foolishly followed Shane and Bryce without bringing anything along. She felt like an idiot, but Shane must have read her mind because he pulled a second water bottle from his pack. "Help yourself."

"Thank you." She drank only a third of the bottle, not sure how many more he had stashed away.

He tucked the open bottle back in his pack, then finished the bottle he'd used for Bryce. Bryce lapped at the water, then lifted his dark gaze to Shane's, clearly waiting for the next command.

"This is Marvin." Shane offered the bag containing the socks and shirt. Bryce sniffed at the items, then looked up at Shane again. "Search! Search Marvin!"

Bryce eagerly wheeled around and lowered his head to the earth, sniffing intently. Then he continued along a path that only the dog could sense.

Bryce led them halfway up a hill, then turned to head east. She huffed and puffed trying to keep up.

The dog had way more energy than she did.

"Good boy," Shane encouraged. "Search for Marvin!"

The dog gamely pushed forward, sniffing along the ground for her grandfather's unique scent.

"I hope we find him soon." Libby gnawed on her lower lip. She was having trouble maintaining her usual sunny disposition. The longer it took to find her grandfather, the more she was forced to accept the possibility that he'd fallen to the ground and injured himself. That he was right now lying in the brush, unable to get up.

Waiting desperately for them to find him.

Hurt but not dead. She refused to believe she may have lost him for good. Her grandfather was the only family she had left. She shared the last name of Tolliver with a guy named Andrew, but there was no relation between them as far as she knew. Her father had walked away when she was a toddler. She had no memory of the man. Her mother had died of a highly aggressive form of leukemia during her sophomore year of college. Libby had left college in Cheyenne, returning home to help care for her mother. But within a few weeks, her mother was gone.

The only thing she had left of her mother was the house. Libby had begged her grandfather to move in with her so they could be together. Grandpa had insisted he preferred living at the cabin. Since she'd gotten the job at the billing department at the hospital, Libby had reluctantly agreed to stay in Cody, using her weekends off to visit and help her grandfather. The arrangement had worked out well.

Until now.

Her grandfather was missing, and her heart ached with the thought of losing him.

Lifting her gaze to the blue sky overhead, she silently prayed. *Please, Lord Jesus, keep my grandpa safe in Your care!*

SHANE COULD SENSE Libby's despair as they continued trailing Bryce's path through the woods. It bothered him to see her this upset.

Not that he could blame her. Knowing how he'd feel if one of his siblings was missing, Shane had gone against his better judgment, agreeing to continue the search. But he remained on high alert in case the shooter was tracking them too.

Poacher? Or someone else? He didn't know and hated feeling vulnerable.

Shane had a carry concealed permit, his side arm tucked in the backpack. At first, he wanted to carry it in hand, but after several minutes of hearing nothing alarming, he'd decided against it. He wasn't wearing his belt holster. At this point, it was more important to keep his hands free.

He kept a wary eye on the time and his compass. He trusted Bryce's nose was taking them to Marvin Tolliver, but Shane needed to make sure they could find their way back to the cabin. Especially if they had to carry Marvin the entire distance.

Maybe he should have called one of his siblings in for assistance. He was fourth of nine siblings, each working with dogs of various specialties. His sister Maya was the oldest, working with a husky named Zion. She was married to DEA Agent Doug Bridges, and they were expecting their first child in mid-December. His brother Chase was married to Wynona, and they had a five-year-old son, Eli. Chase's K9, Rocky, was a Norwegian Elkhound who was a good tracker but had a mind of his own. His sister Jessica was third in line and recently married pilot Logan Fletcher. Jessica's K9, Teddy, was a narcotics dog but could track people too. Alexis was a year younger than he was, and her K9, Denali, had been specifically trained to find dead bodies. Alexis and Denali had been to various disaster sites for recovery missions. Joel and Justin were twins, and their lab K9s were good search dogs too. Trevor was the second youngest, and his K9 was a good tracker as well. And the youngest of the Sullivan clan was Kendra, who worked with Smoky, her large Alaskan malamute.

Any of his siblings would drop what they were doing to assist in the search for Marvin Tolliver. Shane decided that if they didn't find Marvin alive by lunchtime, he'd call Alexis or Joel for backup. He'd reach out to Alexis first because the longer Marvin remained out in the wilderness, the worse his prognosis.

One thing for sure, he wouldn't tell Libby that Alexis's dog, Denali, was an expert at finding dead bodies.

After ten more minutes of hiking, he called for a break. Bryce was a strong, athletic K9, but Shane knew rest breaks were important. "Come, Bryce."

The dog lifted his head and turned to stare at him as if to ask why they were quitting. Then Bryce ran over to his side.

"Good boy," he praised. He shrugged out of his backpack, dropped to the ground, and patted the earth beside him. "Come. Lie down, Bryce."

His K9 obediently stretched out beside him, lowering his head between his paws. Within seconds, Bryce closed his eyes and appeared to fall asleep.

"I wish I could take naps like Bryce." Libby sighed and sat beside him. She tunneled her fingers through her red hair in a rare gesture of frustration. "I don't know what to think, Shane. I thought for sure we'd have found my grandfather by now. It feels like we've been out here forever!"

"I know." He felt bad for her. The only good news was that Bryce hadn't lost the scent trail. "We've been gone just over ninety minutes. I'm thinking your grandfather must have left the cabin pretty early to have gotten this far."

"Yeah, that possibility has occurred to me too." She lifted her face to the sun, sighed, then glanced at him. "I know we're going to find him. I just keep praying to God that we'll find him soon."

He nodded in agreement, although his faith had taken a beating over the years since losing his girlfriend Rebecca two years after they'd graduated from high school, then his parents a few years later. The two blows had hit him hard. His siblings prayed often, and he participated with those prayers, even though his heart wasn't always engaged.

Sure, he wanted to believe his parents and Rebecca were in heaven with God and Jesus, but he couldn't help feeling angry about how they'd been taken from him. Rebecca had only been twenty years old when she'd died in that terrible car crash. Then just when he was coming to grips with that loss, his parents had died in a small plane crash. He still struggled to understand why they'd all been taken far too soon.

Maya would gently remind him that God had a plan for him.

But so far, Shane's only plan was to bury himself in their search and rescue missions.

"I forgot to ask what brand of dog food you need," Libby said, breaking into his dour thoughts. "I've heard that the Sullivan family only accepts dog food as payment for their services."

He waved a hand. "That's true, but we can worry about that later."

She tipped her head to the side. "I have to admit to being curious as to why the only payment your family will take is dog food. It must cost a bundle to keep your dogs in shape to do these missions. And how else are you and the others earning any money?"

He swallowed a sigh, unwilling to get into the inheritance they'd uncovered after their parents' death. "We're fine. Dog food is gratefully accepted because feeding nine dogs—well, ten now that Emily and Owen are at the ranch training their new puppy—takes a ton of food. And I literally mean a ton."

"But what about your salary? How do you pay your living expenses?"

He shrugged. "The ranch is doing okay. We get by." He glanced at his watch, anxious to change the subject. If the locals knew just how much money the Sullivans had in the trust their parents had set up for them, the ranch would be crawling with people trying to get a piece of the pie. They'd all agreed early on not to say anything about the multimillion-dollar trust. The only other people who knew the truth were those who'd recently married into the family. "Five more minutes and we'll get back on the trail."

Libby looked as if she wanted to press more, but just then the distant rumble of an engine reached their ears. Libby jumped to her feet. "Did you hear that?"

"Yes." He rose, too, and his movement was enough to awaken Bryce. His K9 rose, stretched, then lifted his nose to the air. "I can't decide if that was a plane engine or a car?"

"A car? There aren't any roads out here that I'm aware of." Libby slowly turned in a full circle as the low engine noise faded. "I don't see anything nearby. Maybe the vehicle is on a road a mile or so from here."

"It's possible." He tried to envision a map of the area in his mind. This was the first time they'd heard anything resembling an engine, but it occurred to Shane that their poacher may have had a four-wheeler. Some hunters used all-terrain vehicles to help transport elk and deer carcasses through the woods. "If that's our poacher heading out of the area, we'll have one less thing to worry about."

Libby's expression brightened. "That's true. I'm sure that's who's driving the vehicle. It's nice to know he's gone. While following Bryce, I kept expecting the gunman to pop out at us like the boogeyman."

The corner of his mouth quirked in a half smile. "Boogeyman?"

"Yes." She gave an emphatic nod. "Bad guys are always the boogeymen."

Shaking his head, he pulled the collapsible bowl from his pack, filled it with water, and offered it to Bryce. Sensing Libby watching him, he offered some to her. When she shook her head, he replaced it in his pack. Maybe she understood he was trying to conserve their water supply because her grandfather would likely be dehydrated by the time they found him.

If Marvin was awake enough to drink. Based on the silence that seemed to be closing in on them, Shane secretly doubted that would be the case.

Shane told himself to worry about how they'd get Marvin Tolliver out of the woods once they found him. He'd had to haul injured hikers and tourists out of the woods before, so this wouldn't be the first time. Maya encouraged them to carry a tarp in their packs that could be used as a sling just for that reason. With the help of his one-hundred-pound German shepherd, Shane knew they could drag him back to the cabin if needed.

He turned his attention to Bryce. "Are you ready to search? Are you?" He injected enthusiasm into his tone. "It's time to search! Search for Marvin!"

Bryce's tail wagged as he turned and went back to work. Shane had to give Maya credit for her dog-training skills. Between Maya and Ralph Netter, a renowned K9 trainer who'd spent several weeks on the ranch with them early on, each of their dogs were excited to play the search game. Not only did their dogs love it, but they were also exceptionally good at it.

And it was nice to know that he and his siblings had saved hundreds of lives over the past five and a half years.

Thoughts of his parents had him glancing up at the

bright-blue sky. He hoped that if they were in heaven, that they were proud of the work he and his siblings had done.

The way they'd put the ranch trust to good use.

Libby cried out shortly before she crashed to the ground. He rushed forward. "Are you okay?"

"Twisted my ankle." She sighed. "I'll be fine."

"Bryce, come!" He didn't want his dog to get too far ahead. When his K9 turned and rushed back to join them, he knelt at Libby's side. "Let me see."

"It's not bad." She removed her hands so he could examine the injured joint.

Her ankle looked slightly swollen. While not a serious injury, putting additional pressure on the joint could cause the swelling to get worse. "It's going to hurt if we keep going."

"I'm not giving up." Her brown eyes flared with determination. "It's fine. I promise I won't slow you down."

"Yes, you will." He sighed and shrugged out of his pack. "But we can wrap it for now. I'm warning you, though, I can't carry you and your grandfather out of here."

"You won't have to." She looked relieved when he pulled out a small first aid kit. "Wow, you've thought of everything."

He arched a brow as he pulled off her shoe and sock. Then he began to lightly wrap her left ankle. "This isn't my first search and rescue mission."

"How did you and your siblings decide to do search and rescue anyway?" she asked as he slipped her sock back on to keep the wrap in place.

"We wanted to help find our parents." He held up her shoe. "Tie this loosely. The goal is to add support without cutting off the circulation to your foot."

"Got it." She put the shoe on and tied the laces. He rose to his feet, shouldered the pack, then held out his hand. He helped her stand, watching her critically as she took a few tentative steps.

"Are you sure you don't want to turn back?" He frowned, knowing he should insist on giving up the search. Libby might be okay for the next few minutes, but they had a long hike back to the cabin.

"I'm sure. My ankle feels fine." She smiled. "Let's keep going."

Pushing aside the apprehension, he turned his attention toward Bryce. "Are you ready to search, boy? Are you? Search! Search for Marvin!"

Bryce eagerly went back to work, sniffing the clearing for a long moment before moving farther east. Shane wondered if they were still on Marvin Tolliver's property, then decided it didn't matter. As long as Bryce had the scent, they'd keep following.

Until Libby collapsed from pain and exhaustion. Then he'd have another problem to worry about.

Jess teased him about his tendency to express doom and gloom, but it was hard to remain positive at times like this. The only thing worse than Libby hurting herself would be if his dog got injured.

They walked in silence for the next few minutes. Bryce was still following his scent trail, his tail waving slightly from side to side as he trotted through the woods. Marvin must have sweated a lot while he was moving through the woods because Bryce had not once faltered or double-backed, indicating he'd lost the scent. Easy to imagine Bryce sniffing invisible drops of Marvin's sweat that had landed on the ground.

Searches in the summer months were generally easier than in the winter. The family tended to be busier in the summer with the influx of tourists. The fall, too, with hunters coming in from out of state to hunt elk.

It wasn't often that they were called out to search for locals, like Marvin.

Bryce leaped over a fallen log, momentarily disappearing from view. Shane quickened his pace, relieved to see Bryce had landed in a clearing on the other side of the timber.

The dog had his nose pressed into the grass, sniffing intently. Shane glanced around curiously, wondering if Marvin had decided to stop here to rest.

How far had the old man gone anyway? It seemed to him that they should have stumbled across Marvin by now.

Bryce sat and let out a sharp bark. Shane approached with caution, scanning the ground. The grass was pressed down in areas, indicating someone could have been sitting there at some point. He didn't see any more tufts of red thread or any other indication that Marvin had been there.

But then he spotted it. A pair of broken glasses trampled on the ground.

A cold chill snaked down his spine. He glanced over to see Libby making her way toward them. She wasn't limping, but she wasn't moving as fast as she had been either. "Does your grandfather wear glasses?"

"Yes. Why?" Now she quickened her pace. He pointed to the broken glasses and heard her sharp intake of breath. "Those are Grandpa's glasses."

He nodded and drew the rubber ducky from the front pocket of the backpack and tossed it into the air. "Good boy, Bryce! Good boy!"

"I don't understand what happened." Libby held up the broken glasses, glancing around with a frown. "It seems odd that Grandpa would have fallen here in this flat area."

Shane nodded slowly. "I agree, I don't think he fell here." He moved to the other side of the small clearing, then stopped when he saw the tire tracks.

Lowering to a crouch, he estimated the tire width was too small for a car. Not that anyone could have gotten a car in here anyway. But the tire tracks did veer off along a wider trail.

This was where the four-wheeler engine had been. The poacher hadn't just taken off with his dead carcass.

He must have taken Libby's grandfather along too.

3

Trying not to limp, Libby crossed over to see what had caught Shane's attention. Bryce was still playing with his rubber ducky, and she had to admit the large dog was growing on her. Well, as long as he didn't get too close. But the way the K9 had found her grandfather's broken glasses was amazing.

She frowned as Shane slowly stood. "Are those tire tracks?"

"Yeah." He held her gaze. "That was a four-wheeler we heard earlier. I believe the poacher took your grandfather with him."

"But why?" Her heart squeezed with fear. "I don't understand."

"I wish I knew. It doesn't make sense to me either." He stepped closer and placed a hand on her arm. "I'm sorry, but we need to head back to the cabin."

"No, I want to keep going." She couldn't bear the thought of giving up on her grandfather. "We can follow the four-wheeler tracks . . ."

"Not without more help," Shane interrupted. "First of

all, they can go for miles on that thing. We're so far behind now it's not funny. Second, your ankle is hurt. Lastly and most importantly, we need additional equipment and law enforcement backup. Whoever that guy is, he's armed. He shot at us, remember?"

She hated to admit that he was right about the law enforcement backup. She should have called the sheriff's department when she'd noticed her grandfather was missing. It was still hard to believe that Grandpa had gone after a poacher on his own rather than simply calling the game warden. She looked at Shane. "What kind of equipment?"

"We have horses and four-wheelers on the ranch." Shane turned to stare at the trail. "I'm getting the sense the poacher knows this area well. Otherwise, how did he know to bring a four-wheeler? And it's bugging me that he took your grandfather with him. I mean, what's the point of that?"

"I wish I knew." Libby hated the thought of turning back, but hearing about horses and four-wheelers gave her hope that Shane wasn't giving up. "How long will it take to get the equipment here to keep searching?"

Shane pulled out his phone and grimaced. "Having cell service would help. Once I call my siblings, I'm sure they can get packed up and hit the road within the hour."

"That sounds good." Her ankle was sore, so there was no point in arguing. Especially since they still had to hike back to her grandfather's cabin. Sitting on a horse or a four-wheeler would be easier than continuing the search on foot. Safer too. She honestly didn't want Shane or Bryce to be put in danger over this. "There's cell service near the cabin. I talk to my grandfather all the time."

He grunted and turned toward his dog. "Come, Bryce."

The K9 bounded over, dropping the ducky in Shane's

outstretched hand without being asked. She tucked her grandfather's broken glasses into her jeans pocket and followed Shane as he and Bryce set out to retrace their steps.

Her thoughts whirled as they walked. Shane was right that it made no sense for a poacher to take Grandpa with him. Unless her grandfather was hurt? The broken glasses indicated he must have fallen. But why would the poacher care about that? Especially since the poacher knew she and Shane were looking for him? Why not take off and leave them to find and rescue her grandfather?

The niggling concern grew intense as she considered the poacher's goal might be to find another place to dump her grandfather's body. Just because he'd caught the guy poaching? It seemed ridiculous to take things to that extent.

But she couldn't come up with a better theory either.

Libby stepped on a rock, rolling her sore ankle, and winced. Shane pinned her with a sharp gaze. "Let's find a walking stick for you to use."

She wanted to protest, but Shane was already eyeing the tree branches around them. He shrugged out of his pack, removed a small hatchet, and used it to break off a long, thick tree branch. From there, he honed it down, then handed it to her.

"Thank you." She leaned on the stick. "What else do you have in that backpack of yours anyway?"

"Stuff." He gave a nonchalant shrug, then continued heading down the mountainside with Bryce beside him. Now that the dog wasn't in tracking mode, he had his nose up and was sniffing the area with interest. The way Bryce had switched gears from being keenly intent on following her grandfather's scent to enjoying the day amazed her.

The dog was probably smarter than most people.

Using the walking stick helped. She managed to keep up

with Shane and Bryce but couldn't deny a wave of relief when Shane lifted a hand indicating it was time for a break.

Oh, she knew he only took rest breaks for the dog's sake. But she gratefully lowered herself to the earth with a deep sigh. She bent forward to check her ankle. It looked about the same, which she took as a good sign.

"Water?" Shane had filled Bryce's collapsible bowl, then handed her the bottle. She took a sip, then gave it back.

"Thanks." Her stomach was rumbling with hunger, but like her sore ankle, she ignored the physical discomfort. What bothered her more was that her grandfather would be hungry for lunch too.

Would the poacher give him anything to eat or drink? Since she had no idea why the guy had taken her grandfather away in the first place, she doubted his comfort was at the top of the poacher's list of concerns.

"Would you like to share a protein bar?" Shane broke one in half.

"Thanks." She couldn't help but smile as he tucked the empty wrapper into his pack. "I'm surprised you don't have a steak dinner in there."

He cocked a brow, the corner of his lip turning upward in a half smile. Shane didn't smile often, and she couldn't remember the last time she'd seen him laugh. Even back in high school, he tended to be the somber, studious type. "I'm not a fan of cold steak."

She chuckled, despite her worry over her grandfather. "So far, you've had just about everything we need in that backpack of yours."

"That's the goal." He nodded. "I only planned for a day hike, though, so I don't have full camping gear in here. I have that stuff and more in my SUV. We can haul additional equipment as needed the next time we head out."

"Good." She gratefully ate her half of the protein bar. The nourishment took the edge off her hunger, which only made her think of her grandfather again. "I hope the poacher doesn't hurt my grandpa."

"Me too." Shane reached over to take her hand. "Try not to worry. I'm confident Bryce will find him."

She nodded, knowing Bryce was very capable of tracking her grandfather's scent. The issue was how long that might take? The poacher could have taken her grandfather from the four-wheeler to another vehicle.

And if that was the case, she doubted Bryce or any other dog could track her grandfather's scent as he was being driven away in a car.

Her stomach churned, and she did her best to shove the pessimistic thoughts away. There was no point in thinking the worst. She would stay positive. She would continue to pray that God would watch over her grandfather while guiding her and Shane and Bryce to the correct location.

Lord Jesus, please keep my grandfather safe in Your loving arms. Amen.

SHANE COULDN'T SHAKE the cloak of apprehension that had settled over his shoulders as he led the way back to Libby's grandfather's cabin. Something was way off about this scenario. Elderly men didn't wander around the woods for a few hours only to be picked up by a poacher riding a four-wheeler.

If not for the broken eyeglasses, and the broken coffee mug and overturned chair on the patio, he'd suspect Marvin Tolliver was a willing participant in—whatever this was. But that didn't make sense either. If the old man wanted to do something like this, why pick a day he knew his granddaughter was coming?

Shane didn't like mysteries. Especially ones that involved a missing person. He was anxious to reach out to his siblings for their thoughts.

He checked his compass to make sure he was on track. Bryce would find Marvin's scent again if he asked, but he didn't want to set the dog up for disappointment. Marvin wouldn't be at the cabin, and while he could still reward the K9, he knew the dog preferred to find the people he was tasked to find.

They were making good time, despite Libby's ankle injury. He had to give her credit, she hadn't complained once about being in pain. She was pretty and sweet. Maybe once in another life he'd have been interested in seeing her on a personal level. But not anymore. He'd already lost too much.

Dating wasn't even on his radar these days. And someone like Libby deserved better than a gloom-and-doom guy like him.

He wasn't as worried about the shooter now that they'd found the four-wheeler tire tracks. Yet he still couldn't figure out why the idiot had fired shots at them in the first place. It all went back to something fishy going on.

"Your grandfather doesn't owe anyone money, does he?" It was the only theory that seemed to make any sense.

"Money for what?" Libby asked.

"I don't know. Gambling debts?" He had no clue what her grandfather did in his free time. "Maybe a poker game got out of hand."

"I've never seen Grandpa playing poker or any other card game. He's never gone to the Wind River Reservation casino either." She sounded certain. "I would know if

Grandpa owed anyone money. He doesn't. His cabin is paid off; he uses his social security money to pay his property taxes and living expenses."

"Okay, I was just asking."

"I'm sure Grandpa saw the poacher in action and confronted him." Libby's tone indicated she was trying to convince both of them that things weren't as bad as they looked. "Maybe Grandpa did fall and break his glasses, which made the poacher feel bad enough to drive him to safety."

It was on the tip of his tongue to ask why the poacher shot at them, but he held back. Just because he didn't share her positive thoughts didn't mean he wanted to argue over it. Besides, he was afraid they'd learn the truth sooner than later. If the poacher had accidentally killed her grandfather, maybe he'd leave the body somewhere close enough that a hiker might find it.

"If your grandfather is at the hospital, I'm sure they'll contact you." He glanced at her. "I assume you're listed as his emergency contact."

"I am! That's true." Her expression brightened. "I'll call the hospital as soon as we get within cell range."

He simply nodded as they continued hiking. He was about to call for another break when his phone vibrated with an incoming text. Pulling the phone from his pocket, he saw his brother Joel's name on the screen.

Need help?

"We have cell coverage," he announced while texting his brother back. *Yes. I'll call soon.*

"That's a relief!" Libby tucked her walking stick under her arm, pulled her phone from her pocket, and scrolled for a moment. Then she lifted the device to her ear. "Hello, this is Libby Tolliver, is my grandfather Marvin Tolliver there?" There was a brief pause. "No, not as a visitor, as a patient."

Shane stopped near a fallen log, the same one they'd passed on their way up the hillside. He shrugged out of his pack and poured water for Bryce. His K9 lapped the water, then stretched out to rest.

"Oh, okay. Thanks. Will you please call me if he is brought in? I appreciate it." Libby's expression was one of defeat. "He's not there."

"Maybe they're still en route." Shane didn't believe that for one minute, but he hated to see her so sad. "The four-wheeler may have taken him to a car. From there, it's at least an hour or more to get to the hospital."

"You're right." Her smile didn't have the same brightness as earlier. "I had wondered if they'd taken the four-wheeler to a car or truck. I don't suppose Bryce will be able to track Grandpa if that's the case."

He winced, wishing he hadn't brought it up. "Probably not. It's really difficult for any K9 to track a subject in a moving vehicle. There have been cases where human scent is shed through an open window, but usually those are shorter distances, like maybe from a house to a place of business. Not over dozens of miles."

"I was afraid of that." She lowered herself to the ground with a sigh. "There's still time, though. The hospital promised to let me know if Grandpa is brought in."

He almost told her not to hold her breath waiting on that. Again, she was depressed enough without his adding to it. Instead, he pulled out his phone. "I need to talk to my brother."

"Go ahead." Her eyes brightened at that.

Thankfully, his brother answered on the first ring. "Shane, what's going on? I texted you an hour ago."

"Yeah, sorry about that. No cell service. I'm with Libby Tolliver, and we've been tracking her grandfather through the woods. Bryce alerted on several locations, which is great, but it appears her grandfather was taken away by a four-wheeler."

"Taken where?" Joel asked. "That seems odd."

He didn't want to provide a lot of detail with Libby within earshot. "I'd like you and Alexis to head here with at least three four-wheelers. Bring your K9s too." He glanced at Libby who was clearly listening to his side of the conversation. "We can spread out and cover more ground with additional K9 support."

Joel hesitated a beat. "You're concerned the old man might be dead. That's why you're asking for Alexis to bring Denali."

"I think anything is possible. Will you both head out? I'll text you the address. We're east of Greybull."

"Of course, we'll join you. We'll pack additional supplies, too, just in case." Joel, like the rest of the Sullivan family, believed in being prepared. It was a motto that had worked well for them, especially during searches that took place in winter. Heading into the wilderness in the summer had its threats, too, like close encounters with bears and bobcats. But he'd take wild animals over subzero temps any day of the week. Joel added, "Is there anything specific you need? I'm still not sure what level of danger you're anticipating here."

"Food would be great." The half of protein bar he'd shared with Libby hadn't lasted long. "And yes, you should make sure everyone is armed. I'll text you the address. We're probably less than an hour away from Libby's grandfather's cabin."

"Sounds good. You know Anna will take care of us, and

we'll make sure we're armed with handguns," Joel assured him. "Alexis and I are on the way. Stay in touch, bro."

"Thanks, Joel. Will do." Lowering the phone, Shane couldn't deny a sense of relief at knowing more resources were on the way. But his family wasn't all they needed as far as additional support. "Libby, call the sheriff's department. It's time to make an official missing person report for your grandfather."

"Okay." It was his turn to listen as she made the call. She gave her name, her grandfather's name, and briefly described how her grandfather had gone missing. "I called Shane Sullivan, and his K9, Bryce, tracked my grandfather to a location where we found his broken glasses. There were four-wheeler tire tracks, too, so we think he was taken away." She paused to listen. "Yes, I understand that sounds strange, but it's the truth. Please have a deputy meet us at my grandfather's cabin." She held Shane's gaze for a moment. "We should be back in about an hour." Another pause. "Thank you."

He could tell she wasn't encouraged by the conversation. "Hey, it's going to be fine. Making the call was the right thing to do."

"I know. The dispatcher sounded skeptical of my story." She shook her head impatiently. "Like I'd make something like this up."

Shane rose to his feet, then held out his hand to help Libby get to her feet. "We should go. I don't want my family or the deputies sitting around waiting for us."

"I'm ready." She picked up her walking stick with a determined resolve. "I'm anxious to get back out here to search."

"How's the ankle holding up?" He watched her for a moment. She didn't limp, which was good. But he could tell the joint was somewhat painful based on the way she leaned on the stick.

"I'm fine." She pasted a smile on her face. "I'll keep up no problem."

"I know you will. Come, Bryce." His K9 rose, stretched, then trotted forward.

They made good time on the last leg of the journey. When they reached Marvin's cabin, the place looked exactly as he remembered. But he turned toward Libby and gestured to the structure. "Take a look around, let me know if you see anything unusual."

"Unusual how?" She set the walking stick up against the cabin.

He swallowed a sigh. "I don't know. I doubt anyone has been here, but considering everything that's happened, you should double-check."

"Yeah, okay." She frowned, then opened the sliding glass door. "You and Bryce should come inside too."

Sensing she didn't want to be alone, he nodded in agreement. The interior of the cabin was clean and neat. He and Bryce waited in the main living room as she checked the bedrooms. Then she disappeared into the bathroom. A few minutes later, she returned.

"Ah, please go ahead and use the bathroom if needed." Her cheeks went pink as she crossed to the fridge. "Grandpa is well stocked on water too."

"Thanks." He shrugged out of his backpack and eyed his dog. "Sit, Bryce. Good boy, now stay."

The dog didn't move from his position near the backpack as Shane headed to the bathroom. As he used the facilities, then washed up at the sink, he eyed his watch. Hopefully, Alexis and Joel would make good time getting there with the four-wheelers. He wondered if the sheriff's deputies would want to use one, too, and realized he should have asked his siblings to bring all four ATVs.

Too late now. Besides, it wouldn't matter that much. He'd already planned to have Libby ride with him with Bryce taking the lead on finding Marvin's scent. Alexis and Joel could double up. Or the deputy could ride with one of them. They'd make it work.

His bigger concern was to get Alexis alone to explain how he needed her K9, Denali, to search for Marvin without telling Libby that Denali was a cadaver dog specially trained to recover dead bodies.

Bryce might still be able to track Marvin even if he'd been killed and tossed down a cliff. But Denali was the K9 with that expertise, and he didn't want to miss the possibility of finding Libby's grandfather.

Dead or alive.

When he entered the kitchen, Libby handed him a water bottle. He glanced over to see Bryce sitting just where he'd asked him to wait.

"Here, boy." He called the dog over. Bryce immediately came over to stretch out at his feet. He stroked the dog's tan and gold fur.

"I just went grocery shopping for Grandpa, so I can make sandwiches if you'd like."

"I'm okay for now. I asked Joel and Alexis to bring food, that way you don't have to feed all of us." He shrugged. "If you can wait a while, they'll bring plenty."

She hesitated, then nodded. "I can wait." She dropped into a kitchen chair. "I still can't believe the poacher took Grandpa away on his four-wheeler."

"I know. Try not to worry too much." He could do that for both of them. Shane pulled out the chair to sit beside her. "You're sure nothing looks out of place?"

She shook her head. "I don't see anything unusual. Other than the overturned patio chair and the broken coffee mug that I pointed out to you earlier." She waved a hand at the interior of the cabin. "Grandpa isn't messy by nature. If there was something odd, I'd notice."

He had to admit that she was right about that. "Do you mind if I get a bowl for Bryce?"

"Help yourself." She set her injured ankle up on the seat of the chair next to her. "Whatever you need. I owe Bryce a lot for how he tracked Grandpa the way he did."

"Trust me, Bryce likes the search game." He opened two cupboards before he found the bowls. He filled one with water from the sink and set it down for Bryce.

His K9 eagerly lapped at the water, then sat panting. Dogs panted to get rid of the excess heat, they didn't sweat through their skin like people did, and he felt a little guilty for working his K9 so hard.

"We'll let you ride up on the four-wheeler so you can rest," he told the dog. "Okay, boy?" Bryce thumped his tail on the floor in agreement.

"Excuse me." Libby abruptly stood, wiping at her face before heading down the hall. One of the bedroom doors closed with a soft snick.

He frowned, staying where he was, hoping she wasn't crying her heart out in what he assumed was the bedroom she stayed in while visiting. He wasn't good at offering comfort in these types of situations. Restless, he stood and paced the length of the house, then decided to head outside. He snagged his backpack, then gave Bryce the hand gesture for *come*.

The dog didn't hesitate to join him outside. Despite their long trek, the dog seemed ready and raring to go.

"Go on, Bryce, get busy." The Sullivans used the term *get*

busy to encourage their K9s to go relieve themselves. When Maya had first introduced the phrase, he thought it was strange, but now he couldn't imagine using anything else. "Get busy."

Bryce went around the backyard, lifting his leg. Then he finally found a spot to squat. He fished in the pack for his baggies, then cleaned up after his dog. "Good boy."

Bryce wagged his tail, then padded to a spot in the shade, stretching out on the cool concrete.

Leaving his dog there, Shane rounded the corner of the house to check the road. No sign of either the deputy or his siblings. Both parties should be arriving soon.

He turned to head back to Bryce when he heard a scream.

Libby! Shane broke into a run as Bryce began to bark like crazy. As he rounded the corner, he saw a man sprinting away from the cabin.

"Bryce, get him!" The dog sprang up to chase his quarry when the fleeing man turned and fired several shots from a handgun.

"Bryce, down! Get down!" As much as he wanted to get that guy, he wouldn't risk his K9's life to bring him in.

Within seconds, the fleeing man made it to the woods. Another minute passed, and another.

Then he heard an engine roar to life. The assailant was getting away!

There was nothing Shane could do to stop him.

4

———

Seeing the man's head popping up through her grandfather's cellar had scared her to death. Libby had screamed, then wished she hadn't when the guy broke into a run. As she bolted from her room to head outside, she heard gunfire.

"Shane! Bryce!" She wrenched the patio doors open.

"He's gone." Shane was crouched beside his K9, who stared intently at the location in the woods. He glanced over his shoulder to meet her gaze. "I couldn't risk sending Bryce after him when he began shooting."

"Of course not." She didn't blame him for protecting Bryce. "I can't believe he was hiding in the cellar."

"The cellar?" Shane rose to his feet and headed toward the side of the cabin. She joined him, reaching over to close the cellar door. "I didn't notice this earlier."

"I was shocked when I caught a glimpse of him as he emerged from the cellar." She pointed to the window. "That's the room I use when I'm visiting."

Shane nodded thoughtfully. "I would have cleared the

cellar, too, if I'd seen it. But why was he down there? I think he took off on the same four-wheeler we saw earlier."

"But if that's true, then where's my grandfather?" Libby abruptly reached down to yank the door back up. "Grandpa? Are you there?"

"Hold on," Shane said, but she shook off his arm and quickly clattered down the wooden stairs. The cellar was cool and dank.

And empty, except for the canned items her grandfather kept down there.

"He's not here." She felt Shane come down to stand beside her. Then she frowned as she realized the canned goods had been moved around rather haphazardly. "It almost looks like that guy was searching for something."

"Yeah." Shane's scowl deepened. "That takes me back to my original question. Does your grandfather owe someone money?"

"No!" She tried to dial back her annoyance. It was a reasonable question based on the fact that they'd just stumbled over a stranger searching the cellar. "If Grandpa did owe someone money, he never said anything to me. And I would think he'd warn me, especially since he knows I come out to visit every week."

"I don't think that guy took anything with him," Shane said. "The only thing I saw in his hand was the gun."

She shivered, realizing how close they'd come to getting shot for the second time that day. "Do you think it's the same man we saw earlier?"

"I don't know. Let's get out of here." Shane turned to head back up the wooden stairs. Bryce stood to the side of the opening, his dark eyes watching as they climbed out.

Up close, Bryce's teeth looked huge, but she swallowed her fear and offered a weak smile. "Good doggy."

Shane smoothed a hand over Bryce's fur, then reached over to close the cellar door. It dropped with a loud thud. In the distance, she heard a car engine.

"I hope that's the sheriff's department," Shane muttered. "Come, Bryce."

She followed the pair around the corner of the house to see that two SUVs had joined Shane's in her grandfather's driveway. One was pulling a huge trailer. A pretty dark-haired woman jumped out of the first SUV and was quickly joined by a beautiful white and black dog. Libby thought it may be a border collie, but she couldn't be sure. She recognized Alexis from their high school days and lifted a hand in greeting.

"Hi, Libby. I brought lunch." Alexis leaned into the front seat of the SUV and removed a large cooler. "Anna made enough to feed an army."

"That was very nice of her." Libby was touched by their generosity. She was the one needing their help, yet they'd brought food along with the supplies. "Thank you."

"Hey, how about giving me a hand?" The driver of the second SUV must have been Shane's brother Joel. He released the back hatch, and a pretty dog with a glossy black coat jumped out. Instantly, Bryce rushed forward to greet the newcomers.

"Go ahead, Denali." Alexis waved her hand. The collie turned and ran to join the fray.

"I'll be right there," Shane called. "Alexis, this is Libby. Her grandfather Marvin Tolliver is the missing man we're searching for. Libby, my sister Alexis, her dog, Denali, and that's Joel and his K9, Royal. Give us a few minutes to get the four-wheelers off the trailers. Then we'll head inside to talk and eat."

"No problem." Libby was impressed to see the three four-wheelers that were strapped down on the long trailer. Then she turned toward Alexis. "Here, I'll give you a hand with that cooler."

Alexis allowed her to take one end. It wasn't as heavy as she'd expected, but together they carried it inside and set it on the counter.

"I'll grab some plates," Libby said as Alexis opened the top.

"Thanks." Alexis began pulling large containers from the cooler. "Anna made chicken salad, fruit, fresh baked rolls, and there are chips and cookies too."

Libby's stomach growled with anticipation. Then she thought of her missing grandfather who probably wasn't getting anything to eat. For all she knew, her loving grandpa was lying in the brush somewhere unconscious.

"Sounds great." She had to force herself to sound cheerful.

"I know it must be hard." Alexis lightly touched Libby's arm. "We need to have faith in God and in our K9s' abilities to follow his scent. We'll find him."

"I know we will." Libby did her best to shake off the feeling of despair.

Outside, the loud sound of two four-wheeler engines could be heard. Libby moved to the window to watch as Shane and Joel each drove the machines up to the house. Then Joel jumped off and went to get the third one. Shane called his dog, and Bryce came bounding over.

"I'd better get Denali too," Alexis said. "I'll be back in a minute."

Libby set four plates out on the table, along with silverware. Alexis had already set most of the containers on the table, but there were also several bottles of water inside the cooler.

When she had everything open and ready to go, she glanced outside again. Alexis and Shane appeared to be in deep conversation. Joel jumped off the third four-wheeler and called his dog. The black lab named Royal came running toward him. Then the three Sullivan siblings came inside the house.

"Hi, Libby." Joel reached for the chair directly across from where she stood. "Royal, lie down."

The black lab stretched out on the floor, tongue lolling to the side.

Shane took the seat to her right. Alexis dropped into the chair to her left. Each of the three dogs were well trained enough to lie down next to each other.

Libby had honestly never seen anything like it.

"Anna packed a feast," Joel said with satisfaction. When he reached for a roll, Alexis slapped his hand.

"Grace first, remember?" She gave her brother an exasperated look.

Joel flashed an unrepentant grin. "Go for it, sis."

Shane had been silent during all of this and now folded his hands in his lap, looking at Alexis expectantly.

If she was annoyed, Alexis didn't show it. "Dear Lord Jesus, we thank You for this food we are about to eat. We ask for Your strength and guidance as we search for Libby's grandfather. Please keep Marvin safe in Your care. Amen."

"Amen," Libby said. And the two Sullivan brothers echoed the sentiment. "Thanks, Alexis, that was nice."

"Anytime." Alexis lifted the basket of rolls before Joel could grab one. "Ladies first."

Joel sighed loudly. "Hurry up, I'm starving over here."

"You?" Shane spoke for the first time. "Libby and I have

already hiked several miles this morning. What have you done?"

"I waited for you to call me back. That was stressful." Joel helped himself to some fruit, then handed that bowl around the table. The chicken salad went around after the rolls, and soon everyone had plenty of food piled on their plates.

"Not as stressful as being shot at," Shane muttered as he lifted his sandwich.

"I think you need to fill us in on what you know so far," Alexis suggested.

Libby thought the chicken salad sandwiches were amazing, especially the homemade rolls. She nodded, chewed, and swallowed, then began. "I grocery shop for Grandpa every Saturday. When I got here, he was gone. One of the patio chairs was overturned, and his coffee mug was broken on the concrete."

"We left everything in place for the sheriff's deputies," Shane added. "They should be here soon too."

"That's fine; we have plenty of food," Alexis said. "Go on, Libby."

"I called the ranch, your Anna sent Shane and Bryce." Libby quickly explained how they'd headed off into the woods. "Bryce was amazing in following Grandpa's scent."

Shane picked up the thread of the story, giving her time to eat. "We were about ninety minutes in when some idiot took shots at us. We considered the possibility that Marvin had caught a poacher in action and took off to follow him. We wondered if the same poacher was trying to warn us away. We continued the search and shortly after that heard the rumble of a gas engine. Eventually, Bryce found the spot where the earth was trampled down, and there were tire tracks from a four-wheeler. No sign of the machine, the poacher, or Marvin."

"And we found these." Libby tugged the broken eyeglasses from her pocket. "They belong to my grandfather."

"I gotta say, it makes no sense that a poacher would take your grandfather," Joel said between bites.

"Oh, there's more." Shane's expression was grim. "We came back here and didn't see anything unusual. Then I heard Libby scream. Some guy was down searching in the cellar. I sent Bryce to get him but called the dog back when the intruder fired his weapon."

There was a long silence as the Sullivan siblings looked at each other. "Any idea why the guy was in the cellar?" Alexis asked.

"No, but he was searching for something," Libby said. "Cans and jars had been moved around."

"No idea what he was looking for?" Joel asked.

"I wish." Libby sighed. "I'm telling you, my grandfather leads a dull and boring life. He doesn't drink, other than the occasional beer, and doesn't gamble. There's absolutely no reason for anyone to target him like this."

"Maybe they mistook your grandfather for someone else?" Alexis suggested.

"After he's lived here for the past forty years?" Libby shook her head. "I can't imagine that. Unless, of course, this is the work of some newcomer to the area. Someone who doesn't know the locals."

"Anything is possible," Shane said.

"What I can't figure out is how the same guy who took shots at us up on the trail managed to get back here to the cabin without us hearing his four-wheeler." Shane scowled and popped a grape into his mouth. "The time frame doesn't seem to work. It didn't take us that long to get back to the cabin."

"Yeah, and sound carries for a long way out here," Joel added.

"Unless there were two men," Libby said.

All three Sullivans turned to look at her. Shane asked, "What makes you think there's more than one man involved in taking your grandfather?"

"Because like you said, that guy couldn't have ridden that four-wheeler past us, we'd have seen or heard him." She sighed, then added, "I really want to believe the one guy has taken my grandfather to the hospital, leaving the other guy to search the cellar. But I haven't heard from the hospital, so I don't know what's going on. It was just a thought."

"She has a point about two men," Alexis said. "Maybe they split up earlier. One took off with Marvin while the other lagged behind long enough to search the place."

"Great," Shane said in a sour tone. "Now we have to worry about two armed men skulking around in the woods."

Libby fought the sudden urge to cry again. She glared at Shane. "You either keep a positive attitude or stay here while we go out looking for my grandfather." She jumped to her feet. "Excuse me."

She hurried into the bathroom, resisting the urge to slam the door behind her. She closed her eyes, leaned on the sink, and took several deep breaths to get her emotions under control. She refused to let Shane bring her down. She needed to believe her grandfather was going to be all right. That they'd find him very soon, alive and well.

Alive and well, she silently repeated. That was all she could ask for.

"WHAT IS WRONG WITH YOU?" Alexis demanded in a low voice. "Can't you see she needs your support right now?"

Shane grimaced and nodded. "I know that. It's just—you both know the odds are not in our favor. If there really are two men involved in this mess, then it's not looking good that we're going to find Marvin alive."

"You gotta have faith, bro," Joel drawled. "Alexis is right. Doesn't do us any good to have Libby falling apart."

"I'll talk to her." Shane stood, but Alexis beat him to it.

"I'll go." At Shane's narrow look, she added, "Don't worry, I won't mention Denali is a cadaver dog. You're right that Libby doesn't need to know that yet. It's more important that she holds on to her faith that we'll find her grandfather."

"Okay, thanks." Shane was glad she agreed with him on that much. When he'd first explained his intent to keep Libby in the dark, Alexis had argued that Libby should know the truth. But then after he'd explained about the glasses and how Libby had already been through a lot, his sister had relented. He felt bad about adding to Libby's distress by his thoughtless comments.

He was an idiot. Why couldn't he keep his grim thoughts to himself?

Shane had lost his appetite but forced himself to finish the meal. He suspected they had a long afternoon and evening ahead of them. Even with the four-wheelers, he doubted they'd be back much before dark.

Hopefully with Marvin riding alongside them.

"A sheriff's deputy squad just pulled in." Joel waved a potato chip toward the window.

Shane glanced at the hallway where Libby and Alexis had disappeared, then stood. At his movement, Bryce jumped to his feet too. "Come, Bryce." He headed outside to greet the sheriff's deputy. There was only one who'd responded to the call, which he thought was odd. Usually, they sent deputies out in pairs. Then again, summer was the busiest time of the year with tourists flocking to the area.

Recognizing Deputy Paul Holland, he nodded a greeting. "Hey, Paul. Thanks for coming."

"Shane." Paul was a few years older than Shane, and they'd worked together on a case related to a missing hiker last fall. The outcome of that search had been good. They'd found the hiker with a broken ankle but otherwise unharmed. Paul frowned. "I expected to see Libby Tolliver here. She's the one who called the dispatcher."

As if hearing her name, Libby came out of the cabin to join them. Shane was secretly glad she didn't appear to have been crying. Shane quickly made introductions. "This is Libby Tolliver, she's Marvin Tolliver's granddaughter, and yes, she made the call to the dispatcher about how her grandfather went missing. Libby, this is Deputy Paul Holland."

"Deputy, thanks for coming." Libby shook the deputy's hand. "Has Shane explained what happened?"

"Not yet," Paul drawled.

"Come inside," Libby suggested. "Have you had lunch?"

"I could eat," Paul said with a grin.

Shane and Bryce trailed behind Libby and Paul. He'd wanted to apologize to Libby but couldn't find the words. He wished he could feel more optimistic about her grandfather's chances of survival, but he couldn't help expecting the worst.

But Alexis was right in that he needed to keep his trap shut.

By the time Paul had eaten, and they'd filled the deputy in on what had transpired, the hour was going on two in the afternoon. Shane was itching to hit the trail, and he could tell Libby wanted that too.

Paul wasn't enthusiastic about taking the four-wheelers to search for Marvin Tolliver with two armed and dangerous poachers on the loose, but he finally relented.

Shane jumped up as Libby began to clear the table. "Joel, let's get our gear strapped down on the ATVs."

"What can I bring?" Paul asked as he hurried to keep up.

"Your badge and gun," Shane said bluntly. "If we catch one or both of these guys, we'll need you to take them into custody."

"Yeah, okay." Paul grimaced. "Works for me."

Fifteen minutes later, they were finally ready to roll. Shane helped Libby step up onto the two-seater four-wheeler beside him. Alexis drove her own machine, leaving Joel to bring Paul.

"I'll have Bryce to lead the way," Shane suggested. "Denali and Royal can follow along." He gave Alexis a look that indicated her dog would be up next.

"Fine with me." Alexis gave him a tiny nod back. "Let's do this."

Shane revved his dog up, offered the scent bag and water, then gave Bryce the search command. "Search, boy. Search for Marvin!"

Bryce eagerly trotted off toward the woods following the same path as he had earlier. The dog didn't seem to mind that they were retracing steps he'd already taken. Bryce was eager to lead the way.

It was impossible to carry on a conversation over the roar of the engines. The trip was much faster using the ATVs, though, and for that, Shane was grateful. He braked to a stop near the fallen log when Bryce sat and barked his alert.

"Good boy!" He praised the dog and tossed his rubber ducky. Leaving the engine idling, he gestured for Paul to come over. "See this red thread? We think this came from Marvin's red plaid shirt."

"I double-checked earlier, and the red shirt is missing from his closet," Libby said. "I'm sure that's what he's wearing."

"Okay, so we know for sure Marvin got this far," Paul said.

"Oh, we know he came farther than this." Shane turned and mounted the four-wheeler. "Let's go."

Shane didn't linger at the second place where Bryce alerted but pushed on. When they reached the clearing where they'd found Marvin's broken eyeglasses, he stopped. Bryce did his alert again, so he rewarded the K9 and then gestured for Paul to join him.

"See these tire tracks?" He gestured to them. "They're about the same size as the ones on our machines. I'm sure that's the engine we heard."

"I see them." Paul frowned. "And this is where the glasses were?"

"Yep." Shane turned and gestured to the path ahead. "I assumed they took off in that direction." He glanced at Alexis, then added, "I think we should ask Denali and Bryce to keep searching, see if they can pick up the scent trail."

Alexis nodded and told her collie, Denali, to get down from the four-wheeler. She bent over the dog, speaking softly. With the three engines idling, Shane couldn't hear her, but he knew she was asking her to find napoo. Rather than using the word dead body, cadaver handlers used napoo which meant finished, done, dead. It was better to use something that most people didn't recognize, especially when working large disaster scenes.

"Bryce, come." He waited for his K9 to bring his ducky back. "Good boy. Are you ready? Let's search! Search Marvin!"

Bryce wheeled toward the path ahead. Not to be outdone, Denali joined him. The two were searching for different scents, hopefully leading to the same person.

"Shouldn't Alexis have used the scent bag?" Libby asked as he hopped up into the seat and took off to follow Bryce and Denali.

"She used the scent from the clearing," he lied, avoiding her gaze. Obviously, he'd have to tell Libby the truth eventually. Especially if Denali was successful in finding her grandfather's remains.

He wanted to pray that they'd find Marvin alive. Too bad God had stopped answering his prayers a long time ago.

"The dogs are amazing," Libby said in awe, interrupting his dark thoughts.

"Yeah. Good thing they love this game." He kept his gaze on Bryce. It seemed as if the dog was following Marvin's scent, which was good. Maybe they would reach the old man in time to save him.

They followed the path for fifteen minutes, covering the distance quicker than he'd anticipated. Then Bryce let out a sharp bark.

Shane's pulse kicked up as he stopped the four-wheeler and put the machine in park. Then he jumped down to see what had caught Bryce's attention.

His shepherd stared at him intently, as if Shane could read the dog's thoughts. He swept his gaze over the ground and saw the indentation of a heel print in the soft earth.

He frowned, trying to imagine why the poacher/gunman/intruder had stopped there with Marvin. He turned and eyed Alexis, who shrugged helplessly as Denali sniffed the area with interest.

But the female border collie didn't alert the way Bryce had.

"What did he find?" Libby asked.

"Not sure." Maybe they'd stopped for a bathroom break. It was the only explanation he could come up with. There was nothing but woods surrounding them. No sign of a road or a dwelling that he could see. "Good boy, Bryce. Search! Search for Marvin!"

Bryce dropped his nose to the ground and sniffed for a full minute. Then he trotted forward, moving along the path that was occasionally marked with tire tracks from the four-wheeler the poacher had ridden.

He jumped back behind the wheel and put the machine in gear, anxious to keep up. Denali seemed eager to keep moving, too, and he wished he knew which dog would find Libby's grandfather.

The trail turned to the right, then headed downhill. They rode for another ten minutes, following Bryce and Denali.

Then Bryce let out a sharp bark. He'd lost sight of the dog for a moment. He drove up and over the edge of a hill, then stopped.

Bryce was sitting on the ground near a two-track dirt road. Denali was nearby but didn't seem interested in whatever scent had caught Bryce's attention.

He jumped down and crossed over to where his dog waited. There were some crisscrossed footprints in the ground, none as distinctive as the heel print from earlier, but Shane didn't doubt Bryce's nose.

If his K9 said Marvin had been there, then he believed him. "Good boy," he praised, tossing the rubber ducky. But even as he searched the two-track road, he realized the search was likely over.

The tire tracks here were large and wide, belonging to a truck or an SUV. Whoever had taken Marvin had driven the old man out of there.

Leaving them with nothing to go on.

5

———————

Libby hopped off the four-wheeler to join Shane near the two-track road, her stomach tight with fear and dread. She'd been convinced that Bryce and the other K9s would be able to find her grandfather.

But seeing the truck tires on the ground was disheartening.

The rest of the team got off their machines as well, crossing over to examine the area. She noticed Joel and Alexis spread out with their dogs to expand the search of their surroundings. Bryce knew his job was done, as he shook his head from side to side with the rubber ducky in his mouth.

"Can we follow the road?" Libby asked.

"We can take the four-wheelers down the two-track, but does anyone know where it leads?" Shane glanced at Deputy Paul Holland. "Do you know if this goes all the way to the highway?"

Paul shrugged. "I believe so. Can't say that I've been in this exact location before, though. I can say that Highway 14 is to the south of us. If this road doesn't lead to the highway, it could be connected to another parcel of land."

The possibility of finding her grandfather at some cabin lifted her spirits. "Shane? Can we check it out?"

He exchanged glances with his siblings who had joined them after their fruitless search of the clearing. "Sure."

"Thank you." She couldn't tell if Shane was just being his usual grumpy self or if there was a reason he wasn't thrilled with the idea of pushing forward. She told herself it didn't matter as long as he and Bryce got the job done.

"Come, Bryce." Shane waited for the dog to bring the ducky back. He put the toy in his pocket, then gestured to the ATV. "Up, boy."

The dog gracefully jumped up onto the bench seat. She took a step back, wondering if he expected her to jump on a different ATV. But no, Shane looked at her. "He'll sit between us; you'll need to hold on to him."

"Me?" Her voice came out in a squeak.

"He won't bite." Shane looked exasperated. "He's a sweetheart."

"Yeah, with huge teeth," she muttered under her breath. She stepped up and onto the four- wheeler, sliding in next to Bryce. The dog sniffed her curiously, but as promised, he didn't try to bite. She slipped her arm around the back of the dog. His fur was softer than she'd anticipated. "Good boy."

Shane jumped behind the wheel and started the machine. Minutes later, they were back on their four-wheelers and heading mostly downhill on the two-track road.

She held on to Bryce with one hand and the roll bar in front of her with the other. It wasn't easygoing. The two other dogs were running alongside the machines, seemingly full of energy. She understood why Shane wanted to rest Bryce. The dog had worked hard searching the mountainside all day.

Libby didn't begrudge Bryce a break. She just wished his strong jaw full of sharp teeth wasn't so close to her face.

Turning away from the dog, she scanned the area. The thick foliage made it difficult to see any dwellings. She thought there would have to be a driveway of sorts leading to the property, so she concentrated on looking at both sides of the dirt road.

But after a long twenty-minute ride, she could see the highway up ahead. Her spirits plummeted to the soles of her feet.

Whoever had taken her grandfather was long gone.

Shane stopped the four-wheeler, lifting his hand so the others behind him took note and did the same. Doing her best to hide her depression, she was about to slide out of her seat when Bryce turned his head and licked her cheek.

She couldn't help but smile, even as she wiped the moisture away. The big, scary-looking dog was clearly a softy at heart.

"That's Highway 14." Shane jumped down and examined the two-track road. "I see the tire tracks, but it's hard to tell if the poacher was hauling a trailer."

"He must have a trailer, or he wouldn't be able to get the four-wheeler and Marvin Tolliver out of here," Joel said.

Libby noticed Alexis was bent over her dog, Denali, speaking in low tones. Then Alexis threw out her arm. "Search napoo!"

"Napoo?" Libby frowned and glanced at Shane. "Why doesn't Denali search for missing people's names?"

Shane shrugged, his glance moving toward the border collie. "Different training techniques."

Alexis walked into the woods behind Denali as the dog explored the area with her nose. The pair worked for a solid fifteen minutes while Joel and Shane refilled the gas tanks with the containers that were strapped to the back of each machine.

When Alexis and Denali returned, Alexis gave Shane a slight shake of her head. Libby wasn't surprised her grandfather wasn't sitting in the woods nearby and didn't understand why Alexis and Denali had even bothered to search. Did they think the poacher tossed her grandfather out of the truck?

Then realization dawned. Alexis and Denali were searching for her grandfather's dead body.

She turned to ask Shane if that's why he'd asked his sister to come along, but he was peering down at something in his hand.

"Based on my compass coordinates, we should probably drive alongside the highway back to Marvin's cabin," Shane said. "It's a shorter and more direct route than retracing our route back up the two-track and through the woods."

"Works for me," Paul said. Libby could tell the deputy was ready to get back to his regular duties. "I need to check in with our dispatch."

Her disappointment at giving up the search was just as keen as her horror at realizing Denali had been searching this whole time for her grandpa's dead body. But what could she do? Ask Shane and his siblings to drive around the highway looking for a truck pulling four-wheelers?

Why not?

"Libby, are you ready?" Shane looked at her expectantly. She belatedly realized everyone else was back on their respective machines.

"Yes." She stepped back up into the seat next to Bryce.

The dog's mouth was open, his tongue lolling to the side. She slid her arm around the dog's torso and gripped the roll bar. Shane put the four-wheeler in gear and continued down the dirt road until they reached the highway.

He was right about the trip being shorter and quicker. Shane turned right into her grandfather's driveway, pulling to a stop near the trailer Joel had brought from the Sullivan K9 Search and Rescue Ranch.

She slid off the machine, waiting for the others to do the same. Then she stepped closer to Deputy Paul Holland. "Can you put out an alert to look for a truck or SUV pulling a trailer with a four-wheeler on it?"

Paul hesitated, then nodded. "Yeah, I can do that."

She was glad to have that much. She turned to Shane. "I'd like to drive around to look for a four-wheeler trailer too."

Shane glanced at his siblings, then rubbed the back of his neck. "I don't think that's the best use of our time, Libby."

"What do you suggest?" She wasn't going to sit around doing nothing. She pulled out her phone, but of course, there was nothing from the hospital. Frustrated, she stuffed it back into her pocket. "You know what? Never mind. I'll drive the area myself. If I see something suspicious, I'll let the sheriff's department know."

She turned to head toward her pickup truck, but Shane grasped her hand, holding her back.

"Please wait. I'll go with you." He tugged her back toward him. "We'll take my SUV, though, because it's specially equipped for Bryce."

She glanced at the dog playing in the yard with Denali and Royal. The three dogs clearly enjoyed their time together, and she wondered what it was like to live on the ranch with nine dogs all together. Or was it ten now? Hadn't he mentioned something about a puppy?

After being bitten by a neighbor's dog when she was young, Libby had never wanted one of her own. Then she found out the hard way that she was allergic to cats. She hadn't minded not having a pet.

Yet there was no denying that having a dog around added a certain enrichment to life. Just watching the dogs play made her smile.

"Libby?" She glanced over at Deputy Paul. "I need to head back. I've already called in the BOLO related to any vehicles pulling a four-wheeler trailer. I also need a recent picture of your grandfather."

"Good idea." She pulled out her phone, scrolled through the pictures, and found a close-up of her grandpa smiling at her. Seeing his wide grin brought a lump to her throat. "What's your number?"

Paul recited it, and she quickly sent the deputy the photo.

"Send that to us too," Shane suggested. "We'll have the family keep their eyes open for him as well."

As she already had Shane's number, it only took a second to send the picture. Soon Joel's and Alexis's phones dinged with incoming messages.

Knowing the police would be looking for her grandfather helped a little, but she also knew the state of Wyoming was vast, and the poachers could have taken him just about anywhere. She tried to remain positive as Paul turned to leave.

"We'll get these back on the trailer," Joel said as Alexis jumped up onto the closest ATV. "You and Libby can take off."

Shane hesitated. "Yeah, okay. I'll call you later."

"Sure thing." Joel smiled at her. "It was nice meeting you, Libby. We'll head back if you find any leads on your grandfather's location."

"Thanks." She felt helpless as she watched the Sullivan siblings put the four-wheelers back on the trailer. They were leaving, too, just like Deputy Paul Holland.

She swallowed hard, knowing her plan to drive around the state searching for a four-wheeler trailer was probably useless. Yet she didn't know what else to do. She was losing hope of ever finding her grandfather.

And this time, praying did nothing to ease the hollowness in her chest.

IT BOTHERED Shane that Libby looked so defeated. Her normal sunny disposition had taken a beating, and there wasn't anything he could say or do to bring it back. That was the only reason he'd agreed to her idea of driving around looking for a car pulling a four-wheeler. He gestured toward the cabin. "Let's take a quick bathroom break before heading out."

"Okay." Libby led the way inside. Shane left Bryce sleeping outside, knowing they wouldn't be long. Besides, having Bryce on guard duty wasn't the worst idea. The dog would let them know if anyone came close to the cabin.

Deep down, he was convinced the pair of poachers were long gone. Why would they stick around the scene of the crime? Although he still couldn't figure out why the one guy had come back to search the cellar.

He finished first and waited for Libby in the living area. He moved around the room but didn't see anything unusual.

Then his gaze landed on a file folder tucked beside the seat cushion in the overstuffed chair.

Shane glanced over his shoulder to make sure Libby was still in the bathroom before pulling the folder out and opening it. He wasn't sure what he expected, but a DNA ancestry report was not at the top of his list.

With a frown, he scanned the results. There was the usual breakdown of ethnicity; 45% German wasn't exactly a surprise. But then he noticed there was another page that displayed the DNA holder had a female sibling. Was that something Marvin hadn't known?

He was tucking the folder back where he'd found it when Libby returned. "What are you doing?"

He flushed, caught in the act. "Sorry, I didn't mean to intrude on your grandfather's privacy. I just wondered if the file folder was what the guy was searching for in the cellar."

"Why on earth would anyone look for a file folder in the cellar?" Libby crossed the room to take the folder from his fingers. "Besides, this isn't exactly a big secret. Anyone on the DNA site can probably find the information if they know where to look."

He wouldn't, but then again, he'd never bothered with any DNA testing. As far as he knew, none of his siblings had either. He gestured to the file. "Your grandfather didn't know he has a sister?"

"Not until I told him." Libby tucked the folder under her arm. "Let's go. We need to search while we have daylight left."

"Sure." He dropped the DNA issue and led the way back outside. Bryce jumped to his feet when they headed toward his SUV. Using his key fob, he opened the back hatch. "Up, Bryce. Get up!"

His K9 gracefully leaped into the back crate area. He

closed the hatch, then headed around to open the door for Libby, before jogging around the vehicle to get in behind the wheel.

"Your ranch is to the west, so maybe we should go farther east," Libby suggested once they were settled. "I'm sure Joel and Alexis will keep an eye out for another four-wheeler trailer as they head home."

"They will. And the deputies will be looking for it too." He glanced at her as he took the driveway to the highway. "I'm happy to go anywhere you like."

She sighed. "I know this is a long shot. But what else can we do?"

He understood her frustration. He and his siblings had been searching for their parents' wrecked plane and their remains for the past five and a half years without success. There was nothing worse than not knowing what had happened.

Along with not being able to give them a proper burial.

When they reached the highway, he turned left, heading farther east toward the Bighorn Mountains.

"Why didn't you tell me Denali is a cadaver dog?" Libby asked.

He shot her a surprised glance. "How did you know?"

She rolled her eyes. "Napoo? What kind of search command is that? To search napoo? That sounds ridiculous."

He shrugged. "Napoo means finished, done, dead. I guess all cadaver handlers use that term rather than instructing the dog to search for dead bodies, as that's rather grim." He paused, then added, "I didn't want to upset you more than you already were."

"I feel like an idiot for not realizing what Alexis and Denali were up to until I heard her tell the K9 to search for napoo." She turned in her seat to face him. "But I've decided to look on the positive side. Denali didn't alert on anything out on the mountainside, which means it's likely my grandfather is alive."

She was right in that Denali didn't alert during their trip through the woods. Since Marvin had been alive as of that morning, the scent of death would be fresh enough to be picked up at a distance. Unlike searching old sites, like when they'd scoured the mountainside searching for their parents' remains.

"I think you're right about that," he agreed.

Libby relaxed a bit. "I appreciate you trying to spare me the truth about what Denali was searching for, but from here on, you need to be honest with me, Shane." When he didn't immediately respond, she added, "I mean it. I understand search and rescue is your area of expertise, not mine. That makes it even more important for you to let me know what you're thinking."

He glanced at her and slowly nodded "Okay. I'll keep you in the loop moving forward. But you need to help me understand why anyone would have targeted your grandfather in the first place."

She sighed. "I've been trying to figure that out for myself too. I just can't imagine anyone being upset with Grandpa. He's the sweetest man without a single enemy that I'm aware of. He worked construction for years and minds his own business. Why would anyone want to hurt him?"

Having never met the man, he couldn't answer that. Libby obviously loved the guy, but there had to be something more going on here than they both realized. He thought about that file folder he'd found stuck inside the recliner cushions. "How long ago did you do that DNA test on your grandfather?"

"Three months ago, why?" She frowned, then added, "Grandpa doesn't have any other family besides me. He told me he was adopted as a baby and that his adopted parents died when he was in his early twenties. He married my grandmother later in life, around the age of twenty-eight, and they had only one daughter, who was my mom. She in turn had only one daughter, me." She tapped the file folder. "I was thrilled to find out that my grandfather had a sister. I thought he'd be happy, too, but he seemed more shocked than excited."

"Shocked?"

"Yes, I think he convinced himself he was an only child when he was given up for adoption," Libby said with a shrug. "I surprised Grandpa with the results last month when the results finally came in. He told me that it was the best birthday present ever." Her smile faded. "I hope we find him, Shane. I can't bear the thought of losing him."

"We'll do everything we can to find him." The rash promise tumbled from his lips before he could stop them.

"Thank you, Shane." She reached over and squeezed his arm. "I'm so glad I called you."

He tried to look reassuring, but deep down, he feared he'd end up disappointing her. He highly doubted they'd stumble across a truck pulling a four-wheeler trailer with her grandfather sitting in the back seat safe and sound.

Then Alexis's words came back to him. *Have faith, Shane. In this search, God's will shall be done.*

Was his sister right about that? He wasn't convinced. Then again, Shane hadn't really prayed in a long time.

Libby continued to hold on to his arm, the warmth of her fingers radiating through him. And for the first time in years, he found himself wanting to pray for her. And for her grandfather's safety.

"Is that a trailer up ahead?" Libby's fingers tightened on his arm. "Get closer, Shane. Hurry!"

He obliged by punching the accelerator. The SUV surged forward, closing the gap. He had to admit her eyesight was sharper than his because he hadn't noticed the trailer up ahead.

But as they grew closer, the side-by-side long hairy tails swinging over the edge of the trailer had him slowing down. "Sorry, Libby, but that's a horse trailer."

"I guess you're right." She sighed and released his arm. Oddly, he missed her touch. "From back there, it looked like something that could be carrying four-wheelers not horses."

Horse trailers were more common around these parts, but he kept that thought to himself as her keen disappointment radiated off her in waves.

"Keep in mind there are several sheriff's deputies out here patrolling the area." He managed a wan smile. "If there's a guy pulling a four-wheeler out here, they'll find him."

"And if they don't?" She winced, then quickly added, "Never mind. I'm just tired and crabby."

"I think you're holding up remarkably well." He reached for her hand. "We'll keep searching."

They drove in silence for a few minutes. The horse trailer turned off the main highway and took a smaller side road. It occurred to him that if the poachers were smart, they'd stay off the main highways too.

He eyed Bryce in the rearview mirror. The K9 was curled in a ball on the cushion lining of the crate area, fast asleep. The dog deserved to rest; he'd put in a lot of miles since heading out at ten thirty in the morning.

Now the hour was going on five in the afternoon without any hint to where Marvin Tolliver might be. He figured he'd drive until Libby called a halt to the search or until darkness fell.

Whichever came first.

"You mentioned the SUV is specifically designed for Bryce," Libby said, breaking into his thoughts. "Is that mostly the crate area in the back?"

"Yes, the crate area houses a water system that comes in handy when we're doing searches in the wilderness. The SUV itself also has a temperature control setting that will cause the engine to start if the interior gets too hot or too cold for the dog. We try not to leave our K9s inside, but sometimes, it can't be avoided."

"Wow, I had no idea these cars were capable of that sort of thing." Libby looked impressed.

He decided not to point out that with money, anything was possible. Maya had been the one to insist that their K9 vehicles be outfitted with all the bells and whistles, much like the K9 vehicles the police department used. His oldest sister had been a K9 cop in Cheyenne until her K9 had been shot and killed. Then they'd lost their parents, forcing Maya to return to the ranch.

What had started from their tragedy had blossomed into a full-fledged labor of love. Each of the Sullivan siblings had taken their calling to do search and rescue to heart. Even Alexis who, in his opinion, had the most difficult job of all.

Shane slowed as they took a hairpin curve. After yet another turn, he instinctively hit the brake when he saw a black truck and covered trailer parked at one of the lookout areas. He couldn't help but wonder if the driver had pulled over because the truck engine was overheating. He knew from personal experience that sometimes happened while pulling a trailer.

"Stop! That could be them!" Libby cried.

He gripped the steering wheel tightly and slowed even further to turn into the lookout. There were several diagonal parking spots, and he pulled into the very first one, leaving plenty of room between his SUV and the parked truck and trailer.

Libby pushed open her door, but he reached over to grab her arm. "No, Libby. Stay back."

"I need to see if Grandpa is there." She tried to shake off his grip. "Please, Shane."

"I'll go." He reached behind his seat to pull his backpack out. "I have a weapon, you don't. What if the driver starts shooting? What good will you be to your grandfather then?"

Libby seemed to consider that as he pulled his weapon from the backpack. From this angle, he couldn't see the face of the driver. And really, the covered trailer could have anything inside.

Or nothing at all.

"If this goes sideways, call 911 and get out of here, understand?" He pinned Libby with a hard look. "I mean it."

"Okay." She pulled her phone out and set it in her lap. "Be careful."

He nodded, letting the engine idle as he slid out of the driver's seat. Then he leaned in and released the back hatch to let Bryce out. Bryce trotted over to his side, looking up at Shane expectantly. "Search Marvin," he said softly. "Search."

Bryce went to work, sniffing the area. Shane held his weapon at his side as he approached the truck. For the first time in years, Shane opened his heart to prayer.

Lord Jesus, keep us safe in Your care!

6

———

Libby's heart pounded in her chest as she watched Shane approach the driver's side of the truck. Bryce was sniffing the area with interest but hadn't alerted. Shane's shoulders were tense as he moved closer. A wave of doubt assailed her. Shane wasn't a cop, and confronting the driver of the truck pulling a trailer that may or may not house four-wheelers suddenly seemed like a bad idea.

What if the poacher pulled a gun and shot him before he could say a single word?

Trying to be quiet, she opened her passenger-side door and slipped out of the vehicle. Without closing the door, she rounded the door and took a few steps forward, her phone gripped in her hand. She had typed in the numbers 911 so that all she needed to do was push the button to connect the call.

Yet even as she eased closer to Shane, she felt sick at knowing whatever took place here would be over and done before the police could arrive.

The driver's side of the door abruptly opened, causing

Shane to stop in his tracks. She froze in place too. Bryce lifted his head but didn't growl. She took that as a good sign. An older man emerged from the car, squinting at Shane. He wasn't her grandfather but could have been a similar age or a few years younger or older.

"What's going on?" the older man demanded. "What's with the gun and the dog? You planning to rob me?"

"No, sir," Shane said. He tucked the weapon into the hollow of his back, then held his hands up where the old man could see them. "My name is Shane Sullivan. I'm from the Sullivan K9 Search and Rescue Ranch. I'm sorry to bother you, but we're looking for a man by the name of Marvin Tolliver."

"Never heard of him." The stranger's gaze darted toward the dog and then to her. "Don't either of you come any closer. And keep that dog away from me."

Shane's shoulders stiffened even more, but he didn't turn to glare at her. He kept his gaze centered on the driver of the black truck. "Sir, do you have anyone else in the truck with you? We know Marvin Tolliver was taken by someone riding a four-wheeler." Shane gestured to the trailer. "Looks to me like you're pulling ATVs."

For a moment, Libby thought the guy wasn't going to answer, then he shrugged. "Yeah, I got a four-wheeler in my trailer. Taking it to my grandson." The old man crossed his arms over his chest and stood his ground. "I'm alone in the truck. But if you come any closer, I'll be forced to take matters into my own hands."

"No need to worry, I don't want to harm you or anyone else." Shane took a step backward to give the man some room. "I appreciate you cooperating with us. As you can imagine, we're very concerned for Marvin's safety."

"Hrmph." The old man eyed Libby. "I guess I can understand that. But I haven't seen anything unusual. Like I said, I'm taking the four-wheeler to my grandson."

"Come, Bryce." The dog trotted to Shane's side. He took another step backward, giving the older man a nod. "Have a good day, sir." When Shane turned to return to the SUV, closing the hatch after Bryce jumped back in, she hastily ducked back into the passenger seat.

The older man stood there staring at them as Shane buckled his seat belt. Then Shane pulled out his phone and took a few pictures of the truck and trailer before backing out of the parking space.

Only once they were back on the highway did the guy behind them return to his truck. Soon the driver was out of their sight.

Libby was glad the encounter was uneventful but hated knowing they were no closer to finding her grandfather.

"You were supposed to stay inside the SUV." Shane shot her a narrow look. "I'm going to turn around and head back to your grandfather's cabin if you can't follow simple instructions."

"I couldn't bear the thought of something happening to you." Maybe she deserved his annoyance, but she had only his best interests at heart. "You're not a cop, and it occurred to me that if the driver was the poacher, he might shoot first and ask questions later."

"Exactly why you should have stayed in the car." He blew out a breath. "Seriously, Libby, you need to let me take the lead on this. I had Bryce as an added layer of protection. You would have only gotten in the way."

"Okay, okay." She knew he was right. "I can't help feeling disappointed. I thought for sure Grandpa was in the truck."

"Bryce didn't alert, and I couldn't get close enough to see if anyone else was inside." Shane's expression was somber.

"I don't want to believe that guy was lying to us, but I would have liked to see inside the trailer."

She glanced at him in surprise. "He's too old to have been one of the poachers."

"Is he?" Shane shrugged. "Who's to say the old man wasn't working with the poachers in some way? Just because Bryce didn't alert on your grandfather's scent near the truck doesn't mean that guy isn't involved. He could have made up the story about taking the four-wheeler to his grandson. For all we know, he had two machines back there."

Realization dawned. "So that's why you took pictures?" Her heart thudded painfully against her ribs. "You think it's possible the two poachers split up?"

"I have no idea, but I didn't want to force his hand." He held out his phone. "Find Paul's name and send him the pictures. Maybe one of the sheriff's deputies will have more luck in talking to him. They'll run his plate number and hopefully get an address."

She found Paul Holland's name and created a text message to send along with the photos. *Passed this guy on the lookout, please run his license and talk to him?*

The response was a long time coming. *Will do.*

With a sigh, she dropped the phone in the center console. "Paul agreed to follow up with the truck."

Shane nodded. "The local police will likely have more success."

And what if their best wasn't good enough? She swallowed the comment, knowing there was no point in thinking the worst. That was Shane's MO, not hers. Deep down, Libby was sure that if her grandfather was dead, she'd know it. Feel it or sense it in some way.

They drove in silence for a few minutes before Shane

gestured to a passing sign. "We'll stop for dinner in the next town, then turn around to head back to the cabin."

She wanted to argue but sensed she'd be wasting her breath. Maybe she should go back to her grandfather's cabin. Better to be close in case her grandfather was able to get back home under his own power. The poachers may have dropped him off someplace far away to give themselves time to escape without being caught. Grandpa could have caught a ride back to his place.

Maybe he was right now waiting for her there.

The minute the thought flashed through her mind, she realized her grandfather would have called her. She recalled seeing his phone on the charger in his bedroom. Grandpa wasn't good about remembering to take his cell phone with him. Every time she scolded him for not answering when she called, he reminded her that he didn't grow up with a phone attached to his hip the way she had.

"We rode our bikes to our friend's houses," Grandpa would say. "We didn't call, we just showed up. If they were home, we'd head out together. If not, we'd move on."

"What's so funny?" Shane asked.

She realized she was smiling at the memory. "Nothing really. I was hoping Grandpa might be waiting for us back at his place, but he left his phone in his bedroom, so if that were the case, I'm sure he'd call."

"I didn't realize he left his phone behind."

She shrugged. "I wasn't surprised, although it would have been nice if we could have tracked it."

"Not likely to have been able to track it very far considering the lack of cell service," Shane said. "I take it he doesn't wear one of those fancy watches that link to the phone?"

"Nope. His watch is one of those older models that

needs to have the battery replaced every year or so." She shook her head. "I think he's had it for almost fifty years. I'm surprised it still works."

The corner of Shane's mouth quirked in a rare smile. Then he gestured to the road ahead of them. "I'm not sure they have a lot of restaurant selections but let me know where you'd like to eat."

"Carla's Café is fine with me." She was aware of a strange awkwardness between them. Under different circumstances, this could have been considered a date.

Not that she could imagine spending a lot of time with the grumpy Gus sitting beside her. Shane was handsome and nice enough, but his less than enthusiastic attitude was already wearing her down.

She needed someone who had the same faith and sunny outlook on life that she did. Even in the face of her grandfather going missing.

"Carla's Café it is," Shane said, turning down a side street.

"Wait, what about Bryce?" She belatedly realized the dog was in the crate area. Bryce had been so quiet she'd almost forgotten about him.

"I'll feed him first, then he can come inside with us." Shane caught her curious gaze. "In my experience, the locals don't mind. I think that's because our K9s are well trained and generally don't cause problems."

"Or because your reputation is one of serving the public," she pointed out. "I'm sure people here realize they may need your help sometime and don't want to burn any bridges with the family."

Shane shrugged and pulled into a parking space. "That too."

Feeding Bryce didn't take long, and she was impressed at

how the dog sat staring at Shane, waiting for permission to gobble up his food. She glanced around but didn't see anything suspicious. She wanted to check in with Paul but knew that if the police had found her grandfather, they'd let her know.

"Come, Bryce." Shane closed the hatch and turned to head into the café. Libby followed, flushing a bit as Shane held the door open for her.

Not. A. Date.

There were a couple of booths open, so she headed to the closest one. Shane slid in across from her, and Bryce made himself at home under the table. She reached for the menu. When her gaze landed on the pot roast special, she thought of her grandpa. He'd have ordered it if he'd been there with them.

"What can I get you?" Their server placed two glasses of water on the table. Her name tag identified her as Georgina. Her wan expression made her appear to be in her forties, but her curvy figure made Libby feel like a stick. The woman might have had almost ten years on them, but that didn't stop her from smiling flirtatiously at Shane. "You're one of the Sullivans, aren't you?"

"Yep." Shane appeared oblivious to Georgina's flirting. "Libby, you should order first."

Libby bit back a smile. "I'll have the pot roast special." She replaced the plastic menu in the wire holder. "Thank you."

"Same," Shane agreed.

"I'll get those orders in." Looking slightly deflated at the lack of attention, Georgina turned away.

"Does that always happen?" She was genuinely curious. "Does everyone recognize you?"

Shane scoffed. "She didn't recognize me. She took one

look at my dog and made an assumption. I don't remember ever seeing her before in my life."

"Guess your family is somewhat famous." She sipped her water.

Shane scowled. "I guess. But sometimes it's a pain to be the center of attention."

"Are you ever happy?" The question popped out of her mouth before she could stop it. "I mean seriously, Shane, look on the bright side. You have a wonderful family. Siblings who drop everything to offer their assistance if needed." She shot him an exasperated glance. "Be thankful for what you have."

"I am thankful," he protested. A flush darkened his cheeks. "But you're right in that I need to show more gratitude."

She wasn't sure why she was lecturing him and decided to let it go. Their dinners didn't take long, and this time Georgina didn't flirt with Shane as she set their plates down. "Hope y'all enjoy."

"Thanks." Libby didn't reach for her fork but clasped her hands together and bowed her head. After a moment, Shane took the hint and did the same. In a low voice, she said, "Dear Lord Jesus, thank You for this food we are about to eat. And we also ask that You please keep my grandfather safe in Your care. Amen."

"Amen," Shane murmured.

She glanced up at him in surprise. His blue eyes clung to hers for a long moment before he gave her a silent nod, and he reached for his fork.

It suddenly occurred to her that if Shane wasn't so grouchy, she'd be in danger of losing her heart.

THE POT ROAST WAS GOOD. Shane was a little surprised that Libby had chosen the special. Based on her slender figure, he assumed she was one of those who picked at their salads.

Which is why making assumptions is dangerous, he thought with a sigh.

"Do you think we'll hear from the sheriff's department anytime soon?" Libby asked. She'd dug into her meal with gusto.

Reminding himself not to be a pessimist, he nodded. "I'm sure they'll be in touch with you soon."

She arched a brow. "Nice of you to say."

He wasn't overly nice by nature. He preferred to be realistic. Setting expectations when setting out on a search and rescue mission was key. But he knew Libby well enough to know she wouldn't appreciate his honest opinion.

And truthfully, he knew the sheriff's department would only call when they had news. Good or bad.

"If you don't hear from them tonight, you can touch base with them in the morning." He finished his pot roast and reached for his wallet. He did the math and removed more than enough cash to cover the tip. "Excuse me." He stood and headed toward the restrooms.

He hadn't spent this much time alone with a woman in eons and was clearly out of practice making small talk. Shane told himself he needed to make more of an effort for Libby's sake.

She was right to scold him for not being grateful for his family. If they didn't find Marvin Tolliver alive, he knew she'd be alone in the world.

And that was something he couldn't relate to. Shane might be a loner at heart, but he always knew his siblings would be there if needed.

Libby stood when he approached. "My turn."

Georgina rushed over the minute Libby disappeared into the restroom. "Can I get you anything else?" she asked with a sweet smile.

"No thanks." He pushed the cash across the table. "Take care."

"Come back for a visit real soon." Georgina smiled again, but when he barely looked at her, she stuffed the cash into her apron and turned away.

"Let's go, Bryce." He stood and gave his K9 the hand signal for heel. The large dog crawled out from beneath the table and sat tall at his side. "Good boy." He stroked a hand over the soft black and tan fur. "You worked hard today, buddy."

Bryce swished his tail back and forth in agreement.

When Libby returned, they headed outside. He gave Bryce the command to get busy. After cleaning up after his dog, they hit the road.

For some reason, the trip back to Marvin's cabin seemed to take forever. Libby stared down at her phone as if willing one of the deputies to call with news.

"If we don't hear anything tomorrow, will you bring Bryce back out to search the woods again?" Libby asked. "I know it might seem useless, but I can't help worrying that somehow we missed him and that Grandpa is still out there."

Despite thinking that would be a waste of time and resources, he shrugged. "Sure. We can give it another try."

"Really?" Her face brightened. "Thanks, Shane." She reached over to grasp his hand. "You're the best."

He wasn't the best, but Bryce was good, and if there was a chance of finding Marvin, Bryce would be the one to do it.

Dusk had fallen by the time he pulled into the driveway. Because the summer solstice was right around the corner, the area wasn't completely shrouded in darkness. Yet the lack of light inside the cabin gave him pause.

"Stay here. I'll take Bryce in first." The memory of the guy who'd bolted from the cellar was fresh in his mind. He reached for his side arm.

"Okay." When he arched a brow, she flushed. "I promise to wait here."

He nodded and opened the back hatch before sliding out from behind the wheel. Bryce stretched, then bounded forward, sniffing the area with interest. Knowing his dog would alert him to anyone hiding inside, Shane strode to the front door and opened it.

Bryce trotted inside, still sniffing curiously. Shane flicked on lights as he went, relieved to see the interior of the cabin looked exactly the way they'd left it.

The poachers hadn't been back. At least, not yet.

But now that he was standing there, Shane decided he couldn't let Libby sleep here alone. Not when there wasn't a neighbor within miles.

He took a minute to clear every bedroom, bathroom, and closet before heading back outside. He opened Libby's passenger door. "It's all clear."

"Thanks." She jumped out, wincing a bit as she put her weight on her sore ankle. "I, uh, will you call me tomorrow then?"

"I'm staying." He winced at how blunt the words sounded. "What I mean is, I don't think you should be here alone. Besides, it's a long drive back to the Sullivan ranch, and I'll just have to turn around to come back in the morning. I'll sleep on the sofa. Bryce will be fine on the floor next to me. We won't be a bother."

She gnawed her lower lip for a few seconds, then nodded. "Okay. Thank you. That's very kind."

He was tempted to remind her that he wasn't kind but practical, but he swallowed the urge. It wouldn't hurt for him to put some effort into being nice. Libby was going through a difficult time, and the least he could do was offer some support.

"I, uh, just need to let my family know. They'll worry if I don't show up." He turned away, tucking the gun in the small of his back so he could pull out his phone. "Come, Bryce." He stepped back outside with Bryce to call Chase.

When his older brother answered, Shane got straight to the point. "I'm sleeping on Libby's sofa tonight. I don't know if you've been updated by Alexis and Joel, but I may need additional search support in the morning too."

"Alexis filled me in," Chase said. "Did some guy really search the cellar?"

"Yeah." Shane stared up at the stars flickering in the sky. "There's something fishy going on, Chase. It just doesn't make sense that someone would kidnap an old man. What could they possibly want?"

"The cabin and the land?" Chase suggested. "You know as well as I do people will do drastic things in desperate times."

"Maybe, but I'm sure Libby is set to inherit the place if Marvin passes away." Shane found himself shaking his head even though Chase couldn't see him. "I don't think this is about the cabin or the land. I think Libby's grandfather has secrets she doesn't know about. Or secrets she does know about but hasn't told me."

"Another good reason to stick close," Chase said. "If this guy comes back, Bryce will take him down."

"Yeah, except the last time the idiot fired several shots to keep us back." The near miss had concerned him. "But

Bryce is a good watchdog for sure. I'll let you know if anything changes. Thanks, Chase."

"Be safe." His brother ended the call.

Shane watched as Bryce trotted around the yard lifting his leg to mark his territory. Shane opened the back hatch and pulled out the backpack he'd used earlier that day. Bryce would need food in the morning, plus water for tonight. He slammed the hatch, waited for the dog to finish up, then headed inside.

Libby had left a pillow and blanket on the sofa. Then he noticed she'd folded a second blanket on the floor for Bryce. Her thoughtfulness made him smile.

"Do you need anything else?" Libby asked, hovering in the kitchen. "I'm sorry, but I couldn't find a spare toothbrush."

"That's okay." He set the pack down. "Bryce has one in the backpack I can use."

Her brown eyes widened, then a wide smile bloomed on her face. "Is that a joke? You made a joke?"

"Apparently not a good one if you have to ask." He raked his hand through his hair, feeling like an idiot. So much for trying. "Never mind. Good night, Libby."

"Good night, Shane." She turned and disappeared down the hallway leading to the bedrooms. He didn't notice her limping and hoped her ankle would be back to normal come morning.

Shane set his weapon on the end table, dropped onto the sofa, and removed his hiking boots, giving her time to get settled before padding to the bathroom. Bryce really did have a toothbrush in the backpack, but Shane had no intention of sharing it. He turned off the lights as he returned, then stretched out on the sofa.

"Here, Bryce." He patted the pallet Libby had made for

the dog. Bryce sniffed it, then made a circle before curling up and closing his eyes. "Good boy," he murmured.

He repositioned the pillow behind his bed and covered himself with the light blanket. The sofa wasn't bad, a tad short, but he'd slept in worse places. It wasn't the strange surroundings that kept him awake.

It was Libby and whatever had gone down today with her grandfather's disappearance.

He couldn't toss and turn, so he tried to relax the muscles in his body. The trick must have worked because Shane awoke to the low growl rumbling from deep within Bryce's throat.

He jackknifed into a sitting position, blinking to peer through the darkness. The low, constant growl was a warning.

Shane reached for the gun and shoved his feet into his hiking boots. He rose and moved through the kitchen, listening for whatever had caught Bryce's attention.

Suddenly Bryce jumped to his feet and let out several sharp barks. A hint of movement outside the patio doors caught his attention. Shane bolted across the room, yanked open the sliding glass door, and shouted, "Stop!"

Of course, the guy didn't stop. He ran toward the woods.

"Get him!" Bryce didn't need additional encouragement. His K9 raced through the opening, covering the distance in the blink of an eye.

Shane followed his dog, again praying the intruder wouldn't shoot. The darkness made it difficult to see clearly, but he shouldn't have been surprised to hear an engine roar to life.

"Get him," he shouted again, hoping Bryce would stop the guy from escaping. But the engine roar only grew louder, then faded as the intruder disappeared.

"Bryce! Come!" Fear lanced through him as he swept his gaze over the area. Then Bryce was bounding back toward him. Relief made his knees go weak, and he dropped to the ground to hug his dog. "Good boy. Are you okay? Are you?" He ran his fingers over the shepherd's pelt, breathing a sigh gratitude when he didn't find any injuries.

Then Bryce dropped something into his palm. Shane stared down in surprise, realizing it was a strip of denim from what looked like the bottom of a pant leg.

From the intruder? "Good boy," he repeated. It wasn't much, but the scrap of clothing would be enough to use as a scent source.

Maybe heading back out into the woods come morning was a good idea. Searching for the guy who'd tried to break into the cabin might lead them to Marvin.

7
———

Bryce's barking dragged Libby from her nightmare. Or maybe the dog was part of her dream, she wasn't sure. Stumbling from the room, she came to an abrupt stop when she noticed the patio doors were open.

"Shane?" Her voice sounded like a croak. She tried again. "Shane!"

"We're coming." There was a slight pause, then she heard, "Good boy, Bryce. Good boy!"

Her heart settled into a normal rhythm as Shane and Bryce approached the patio. Bryce appeared satisfied with a job well done as he trotted into the cabin. Shane stepped over the threshold, sliding the patio door closed behind him.

"Was someone out there?" She frowned as she noticed he had a gun in one hand and something dark blue in the other.

"Yeah, and Bryce managed to bring a piece of his jeans back." Shane held it up for her to see. "Do you have a plastic bag I can use?"

"Um, sure." She turned into the small kitchen and

opened drawers until she found some freezer bags. She held it open so he could drop the scrap of denim inside. It appeared to be the lower hem of a pant leg. She imagined it had been frayed already, and when Bryce chomped down on it, the fabric had pulled free.

"Thanks." He took the bag and glanced at his dog. "Bryce heard the intruder outside before I did. I sent Bryce after him, but I heard the rumble of an engine. Bryce only got a small piece of him."

"I can't believe the poacher came back." She dragged her fingers through her hair. "I don't understand what he hoped to find."

"I'm not sure either, but there must be a reason he risked showing up here." Shane bent to stroke his dog. "I'm glad we stayed. I'll see if Bryce can follow the scent trail in the morning. Maybe we'll learn something new."

"I'm glad you stayed too." She shivered, wondering what might have happened if Shane and Bryce hadn't been there. Especially the dog who'd alerted them to the danger. "It would be good to learn something new. None of this makes any sense."

"Agree." Shane pinned her with a look. "Could this guy be looking for the DNA file folder?"

The possibility hadn't occurred to her. "I don't see why that would be of interest."

"I don't either, but there's something more going on here than we realize." Shane dropped down onto the sofa. "I just can't shake the feeling that these guys have targeted your grandfather for a specific reason. And not because they were poaching on his land."

"Okay, but if that's true, I'm as much in the dark as you are." She crossed over to sit beside him. Bryce nudged her knee, and she cautiously stretched out her hand to pet him.

His soft fur belied his scary teeth. The fact that Bryce had gotten close enough to rip some fabric from the intruder's jeans was amazing. "I'm glad you weren't hurt, boy," she murmured.

"Me too. It's always a risk to send a K9 out to take down a fugitive," Shane said somberly. "If the guy hadn't jumped on a four-wheeler, I'm sure Bryce would have been able to hang on to him."

"I can't imagine driving a four-wheeler through the woods in the middle of the night." She frowned. "How can he see where he's going?"

Shane's blue eyes widened. "Good point, Libby. He must be wearing night-vision goggles of some kind to avoid running into trees and brush. Maybe we should be looking at someone with military connections."

"I don't know how that helps us." She tried not to feel dejected. "We'd need to know his name before we can ask the police to dig into his military history."

"Every little bit of information counts. We know more today than we did yesterday, right?" Was it her imagination, or was Shane trying to pump up her spirits? That he bothered to make an effort to put a positive spin on things touched her heart. He picked up the bag containing the strip of denim. "I was planning to use this as a scent source for Bryce. Now I'm wondering if we should try to have it tested for DNA."

"That will take too long." She wanted to find her grandfather in the next few hours, or a day at the most. Not in a few weeks or even a month. "I'd rather we use it as a source for Bryce to track first." If that didn't work? The image of Denali, Alexis's K9, flashed in her mind.

No, she wasn't going there. She needed to believe her grandfather was still alive.

Shane nodded slowly. "I'm inclined to agree with that approach. I just don't want to miss anything obvious."

Nothing about her grandfather's disappearance was obvious. A wave of despair hit hard. Not only had her grandfather been taken away, but twice now, the same men who'd abducted him had returned to the cabin.

To find what? A DNA report? That made no sense.

"I left it in your SUV." When Shane looked confused, she added, "The DNA report. I left it in your SUV."

"Oh, right. Well, the vehicle is locked and equipped with an alarm, so if anyone tries to get inside, we'll be alerted." He glanced at his watch. "It's four in the morning. You should try to get more sleep."

A remnant of her nightmare flashed in her mind. "I dreamed we found Grandpa tied up in a cave, and when we tried to rush to the rescue, one of the bad guys shot him." She shivered. "It was horrible."

"Just a dream, Libby." Shane reached for her hand. "I'm sure it was scary, but it's only a dream."

She clung to his hand. "I can't bear to think about what these guys are doing to my grandfather."

"Try not to imagine the worst," Shane said. "Maybe they're just holding him someplace far away so they can come back to search the cabin."

"Maybe." She wasn't sure that scenario was any better. "What happens if they find what they're looking for?"

"I can't answer that," Shane admitted. "But you're the one who told me to have faith in God, remember?" The corner of his mouth ticked up in a half smile. "Thanks to you, I prayed for the first time in a long time yesterday."

"Really?" She turned on the sofa to face him, searching his gaze. "I'm glad to hear that."

He looked down at their joined hands. "For a long time

now, I've been too focused on the losses in my life, rather than on the blessings I've been granted."

"Rebecca and your parents."

"Yes." He hesitated, then added, "Working search and rescue has reinforced the fact that lots of people suffer loss. I'm nothing special."

"I think you're special." She couldn't help but smile when he glanced up at her in surprise. "I mean it, Shane. You and Bryce are a special team. And I know you'll be the one to find my grandfather."

"I hope so." He sounded cautious as if he didn't want to over promise. "Are you sure you don't want to try to get some sleep?"

"I'm wide awake now." She belatedly realized Shane might be hinting that he needed to sleep. "Why don't you stretch out on the bed in my grandpa's room? I'm sure he won't mind."

"No need. I'm up now too." He gently squeezed her hand, then released it. She missed his warmth, then told herself to stop imagining a closeness between them that wasn't there. He rose, and Bryce looked up at him as if anticipating they might be heading out soon. "I'll borrow your bathroom, if you don't mind."

"No problem. I'll start the coffee." She rose to make her way to the kitchen. Her ankle felt better, and she was secretly relieved the injury wouldn't hold her back from participating in the search. She noticed Bryce stayed in the living room, stretched out on the blanket she'd set out for him.

After starting the coffee, she poked around in the fridge. Thanks to her grocery trip, there was plenty of eggs, bacon, and toast for breakfast. She frowned, wondering if her grandfather had been given anything to eat. He'd been gone for almost twenty-four hours now.

Even she knew that the longer he was gone, the less likely they would find him alive. As Shane mentioned, though, it was likely the bad guys were keeping him for a reason. She placed the eggs, bacon, and butter on the counter, then stood for a minute looking around the living room.

Had her grandfather hidden something there? She knew he didn't have a lot of money, so it couldn't be anything of real value.

Could it?

She turned away and began frying the bacon. Maybe when they'd finished eating, she'd search the cabin. It didn't sit well to invade her grandfather's privacy, but if there was something there to use as a bargaining chip to get him back, she'd take the risk.

And beg for forgiveness later.

Shane emerged from the bathroom showered and looking more handsome than ever. She poured him a cup of coffee, which he accepted with a nod. "Thanks. Come, Bryce."

She watched as he took his dog out the patio doors. There was no reason to be so hyperaware of him. It had been a long time since she'd dated anyone. The last guy had decided to skip town to hit the rodeo circuit. She told herself she was better off without him since leaving wasn't an option. Not when she had her grandfather to care for.

Besides, Tommy hadn't exactly invited her along. No doubt he'd been looking forward to mingling with the rodeo bunnies that clustered around the shows.

Deep down, she was forced to admit she didn't care about Tommy's decision to move on. She'd missed having someone to be with, but not Tommy in particular. Things hadn't been that serious between them. He was a nice enough guy, but he was always looking for something more.

Something bigger and better.

And why was she even thinking about her lack of a love life? Nothing was more important than finding her grandfather.

While Shane was outside with Bryce, she took a turn in the bathroom. Feeling better, she refilled her coffee mug and continued cooking the bacon.

After another five minutes, though, she grew concerned. What was taking Shane so long? What was he doing with Bryce in the backyard? Hard to imagine he'd started the search for the bad guy without telling her.

Finishing with the bacon, she moved to the patio doors. "Shane?"

"Coming!" She was surprised to see him and Bryce emerging from the woods. He had asked Bryce to start his search.

"Don't leave without me," she said, as Shane and Bryce approached. Shane downed the last of his coffee before reaching the patio. "My ankle is much better today. I want to go with you when you ask Bryce to search for the bad guy."

"I didn't ask Bryce to do anything yet, I only went to look for tire tracks," Shane said. "I found an imprint in the dirt, and it looked similar to the one in the clearing where we found your grandfather's glasses."

"Did you think he was driving something other than the four-wheeler?"

"He could have been on a dirt bike." He shrugged and crossed to the backpack. "Something like that may be easier to use in the woods."

"Interesting." She noticed he pulled out doggy dishes for

Bryce. The large shepherd sat tall, clearly anticipating his breakfast was near. "Um, how do you like your eggs?"

"Over easy or sunny-side up, whichever is easier for you." He scooped dog food into one bowl, then carried them both to the kitchen to fill the second bowl with water. Bryce hadn't moved an inch, but his dark-brown eyes seemed to bore into Shane as he waited. Shane set the dishes down in the corner of the room, then said, "Come. Go ahead and eat, Bryce."

The dog shot across the room, attacking his food dish with exuberance. She smiled as water sloshed over the edge and onto the floor.

"He's something." Shaking her head in amusement, she turned back to the stove. Shane was close enough to be a distraction.

"I can help," Shane offered. "What do you need?"

"Take care of the toast." She cracked eggs into the frying pan, doing her best to ignore his presence. "Are you planning to ask your siblings to help with the search today?"

He shrugged. "I was thinking we'd head out with Bryce first, see how that goes. I hate to drag them out for another day of finding nothing."

"Okay." She wasn't going to argue since heading out bright and early suited her just fine. She looked out the window at the woods beyond.

We're coming, Grandpa. Hang in there, we're coming!

Shane buttered toast, struck by the easy camaraderie between him and Libby. He wasn't sure when their relationship had shifted from mere acquaintances to friends.

Or more?

No, thinking along those lines was dangerous. Libby was only leaning on him now because she trusted Bryce's ability to find her grandfather. Once they'd found Marvin, their time together would be over.

And why that was a depressing thought, he had no idea. He wasn't looking for anything more.

Once they were seated at the table with Bryce stretched out on the floor at his feet, Libby said, "I'd like to say grace."

"Okay." He reached for her hand, then paused. When she smiled and took his hand, he realized his mistake.

He liked holding her hand, more than he should.

"Dear Lord Jesus, we thank You for this food we are about to eat. Please keep my grandfather safe in Your loving arms and guide us to finding him. Amen."

"Amen." He was humbled by her faith and felt bad for having turned his back on Him for the past few years.

"I was thinking I should take Grandpa's shotgun along," Libby said, breaking into his thoughts.

He gave her a long look. "Do you know how to use it?"

"Aim and shoot, right?" She flushed, then shrugged. "It's been awhile since I used it, but considering what we faced yesterday, I'd feel better having a weapon."

"Your grandfather doesn't own any handguns?" He wasn't sure he wanted her to carry a rifle. Even though her ankle seemed better, the longer gun would be unwieldy.

"I don't think so." She frowned. "Although I guess I could look."

He wished he'd have asked Joel or Alexis to leave a weapon behind. "Don't worry about it. I'm armed, and we have Bryce." He didn't add that if the bad guys took aim at them again with a rifle, both the shotgun and handgun would be useless.

This was the new Shane, keeping his dour thoughts to himself.

"I'll look around quick before we go." She finished her breakfast and jumped to her feet. "It won't take long. The cabin isn't that big."

"I'll clean up." He didn't mind pitching in to help. His oldest sister, Maya, had made sure everyone carried their weight when it came to ranch chores. They had a house-keeper, Anna, but when it came to the dogs, the horses, the equipment, and everything else that was required to keep a ranch running, everyone did their fair share.

"Thanks, Shane." She flashed a smile, then disappeared down the hallway. He heard the bedroom door open and shut.

Bryce didn't jump up to follow, maybe sensing that he'd be put to work soon enough. Shane quickly filled the sink with sudsy water and took care of the dishes, stacking them in the second sink to air dry. Then he rifled through his backpack to find his belt holster. The one he hadn't used yesterday.

He wouldn't make that mistake again.

When Libby emerged, she held a shoebox in her hands. "I didn't find a gun, but I did find a box of old photos and newspaper clippings. It's rather strange, as Grandpa never showed them to me."

"No secret stash of cash, huh?" He was mostly joking.

"Nope." She set the box on the kitchen table. "I'll go through them later. I didn't find a backpack to use to help carry stuff either."

"I'll carry our gear. I'm used to hiking with a heavy pack." He pulled Bryce's vest out and strapped it around his K9's torso. "Besides, most of the stuff I'm bringing along is for my dog."

"That reminds me. I found some protein bars and a couple of water bottles." She opened a cupboard and removed a box, then pulled the bottled water from the fridge. "Do you have room in your pack?"

"Yeah." He stuffed four protein bars and two bottles of water in the large middle pocket. After double-checking to make sure he had both bags of scent clothing, he slung the backpack up and settled it across his shoulders. He slipped the .38 into his holster, then picked up the bag containing the denim strip. "Come, Bryce."

The dog trotted beside him as they headed out back. In the middle of the yard, he knelt and offered the scent bag. "This is Bad Guy. Search! Search for Bad Guy!"

Bryce buried his nose in the bag for a long sniff. Then he wheeled and began trotting across the grass toward the woods. Shane rose to his feet and quickly followed.

He'd expected Bryce to follow the same path as yesterday, but apparently, the scent trail was stronger in a different direction because Bryce swerved to the left, taking a sideways route into the woods.

Libby hurried to catch up. "Do you see any evidence he's been here? Like more tire tracks?"

"Just the ones I found earlier." He kept a wary eye on Bryce as they moved through the woods. "Stay alert and let me know if you see anything suspicious."

"I will."

Heading out in the early morning hour was nice as the sun wasn't beating down on them, and the air was cool and refreshing. If not for the worry lines etched in Libby's brow, they could have enjoyed the outdoors.

Bryce moved with a sense of energy and determination. Almost as if the dog understood that today they were hunting a bad guy rather than searching for someone who was lost. Maya always cautioned them how their dogs could pick up on their handler's emotions.

They walked in silence until Bryce stopped, made a circle, and doubled back.

"Did he lose the scent?" Libby asked breathlessly.

"Give him a minute." Considering the bad guy was on a motorized vehicle, it wouldn't be unusual for Bryce to lose track of the scent. "Search for Bad Guy," he called encouragingly.

Bryce went back to sniff at a specific spot, then veered to the right. Bryce moved slowly at first, but after a few minutes, it was clear his K9 was back on the trail.

"Makes me wonder if the bad guy drove back and forth in an effort to throw Bryce off track," Libby said.

"Could be." Shane squinted and paused beside a soft spot in the ground. "There's another tire impression here too."

"Same as the others?" She came up to stand beside him. "I have to be honest, I can't tell the difference."

"I'm not an expert, but they look the same to me." He pulled out his phone and found the picture he'd taken yesterday. Kneeling down, he compared the two images. "See?"

She nodded and scanned the area. "Do you think he rode the four-wheeler all the way to the road?"

"It's hard to say." He repositioned the pack and set off after Bryce. "The way this guy keeps showing up at the cabin makes me think he's sticking close."

Her eyes widened with a hint of apprehension. "If he's still out here, he could hear us coming."

"Yeah." He glanced at her. "Stay behind me as much as possible."

She swallowed hard and nodded.

"Search, Bryce," he called. Not that his K9 needed any encouragement. The dog paused a few times to sniff but then kept going.

Shane hiked for a solid forty minutes before stopping to take a break. Bryce didn't appear tired, but he shrugged out of his pack to pour some water into a collapsible bowl. Bryce lapped at the water, then looked up at him, panting.

"You're doing great, buddy," he assured him. "Lie down."

Bryce stretched out on his belly, still panting.

"None of this looks familiar," Libby said as she sat beside him. She stroked a hand over Bryce's fur almost absently, and Shane was pleased that her early fear of the dog seemed to have vanished. "I'm not sure how you manage not to get lost."

"My oldest brother, Chase, was a hunting guide prior to our parents passing away." He pulled the compass from his pocket and showed it to her. "Chase drilled us on using a compass to find our way, even sending us out in the middle of the night to search for each other as a test."

"Sounds scary."

"Not really. It's more a matter of survival." He cast a glance around the woods, then checked the compass. "We're about a hundred yards from the path we took yesterday. I'm hoping this leads to something other than the clearing."

"Me too." She sighed. "I don't want this to be for nothing."

He fought the urge to hug her. When their rest break was over, he rose to his feet and offered her a hand. "Let's keep moving."

She stood too. "I'm ready."

"Search, Bryce. Search Bad Guy." He offered the denim scrap of cloth, but Bryce barely sniffed it. The K9 seemed to be telling him he knew what to do.

Bryce lowered his head to the ground, then set off at a brisk trot. After a few minutes, Bryce turned north. The incline wasn't bad, but Shane was having trouble imagining the bad guy taking the four-wheeler up this way.

"Seems rather steep," Libby murmured.

"I know." He shrugged, quickening his pace to keep up with his K9. "We have to trust Bryce."

The incline leveled out after a few yards. He glanced behind them, a little surprised at how far they'd climbed. Sweeping his gaze over the ground, he looked for more tire tracks. The pine needles were too thick, though, and the earth revealed nothing indicating the bad guy had come this way.

Ten minutes later, Bryce broke into a trot. Shane's pulse kicked up, and his hand went to his weapon, half expecting to see the bad guy stepping out from behind a tree.

Instead, Bryce turned toward an outcropping of rocks. Then the dog abruptly sat and let out a sharp bark.

His alert! Shane pulled his gun and approached with caution. When he grew closer, he noticed there was a shallow cave opening on the other side of the rock.

"Bryce, stay." He wanted to reward his dog for the find, but he needed to be sure the bad guy wasn't hiding inside. He ducked and stepped into the cave opening. There was a small fire pit there, and several scuff marks in the dirt.

Then he saw a piece of a zip tie partially embedded in the dirt. Shane was sure Marvin and the bad guy had recently been there.

But where were they now?

8

———

Hearing Bryce's bark, Libby hurried forward, slipping a bit as she rounded the rock. There was no sign of Shane at first, just Bryce sitting straight and tall, but then she noticed the cave.

Heart thumping wildly, she edged closer and ducked inside. Shane was kneeling on the ground, picking something up from the dirt.

"What did you find?" She couldn't tell what he had in his hand.

He hesitated, then reluctantly showed her the narrow strip of plastic. She frowned, then realization dawned.

"A zip tie?" Her voice sounded hoarse to her own ears. "You think it was used to bind Grandpa's wrists together?"

"Could be." He grimaced as he stood. "All we can do is bring it back to show the sheriff's deputies."

She swallowed hard, trying not to imagine her grandfather sitting with his wrists tied together. Turning, she glanced around the shallow opening of the cave. There appeared to be a small fire pit, but nothing else. "I'm trying to understand the timeline here. Grandpa's glasses were found in the clearing where there were clear tire tracks from a large vehicle." She threw her arm wide. "How long did they keep him here?"

"I was trying to piece that together too." Shane stepped past her, leaving the cave. She followed, watching as he pulled the rubber ducky from his pocket and tossed it to Bryce. "Good boy!"

Bryce leaped into the air to catch the ducky, then ran around the woods. The dog's antics never failed to make her smile.

Even now, despite knowing her grandfather had been confined with zip ties.

Shane pulled out his compass. "The clearing where we found the glasses is southeast of here." He met her gaze. "We don't know for sure when your grandfather was taken or lured into the woods. But I think he was brought here first. Then when the bad guys discovered we were searching for him using Bryce, they moved him to the clearing."

"Two men for sure." She could easily imagine the scenario Shane described. "One to bring the truck up to the clearing and the other to bring Grandpa from this cave down to meet him using the four-wheeler."

"At least two men," Shane agreed. "Maybe more. Although I have to admit, without knowing the motive, it's difficult to understand why so many are involved."

She shook her head. "I wish I knew why they took him too. The only thing of value that he has is the cabin and the land."

"And you would be the one to inherit if something happened to your grandfather," Shane said.

For a horrible moment, she thought he was accusing her of being involved. "I didn't—"

"I know you're not responsible," Shane quickly added.

"I'm stating a fact. These guys must know about you, so taking your grandfather in some scheme to get control of his property doesn't make any sense."

She relaxed and nodded. "That's true. Grandpa told me I would inherit the place when he was gone. I've been asking him to sell it outright to move in with me." She abruptly turned toward Shane who was taking the rubber ducky from Bryce. "Could that be it? They took Grandpa to convince him to sell?"

"That's a bit extreme." Shane stuffed the ducky into his pocket. "And honestly, any legal transaction done under duress wouldn't hold up in court."

"Maybe the goal is to avoid court."

"Hey, we'll find him," Shane said encouragingly. For a guy who seemed to expect the worst at every turn, he was strangely cheery. "I'll give Bryce another search command. Maybe he'll take us to another new location."

She was so touched by his caring that she crossed to his side and lifted up onto her tiptoes to kiss his cheek. "Thanks, Shane."

"You're welcome." His cheeks flushed, but he quickly turned toward his K9. He shrugged out of his pack, poured water into a bowl, and offered it to the dog. Bryce lapped at the liquid, then stared expectantly at Shane. After tucking the collapsible bowl away, he offered Bryce the scent bag. "This is Bad Guy. Search! Search Bad Guy!"

Bryce briefly sniffed the bag, clearly already having the scent locked in his mind. Then he lowered his nose to the ground and moved down the side of the hill. Shane stood, shouldered his pack, then headed after the dog.

Libby followed, searching the ground for signs the four-wheeler had gone this way. The ground was too covered with pine needles to reveal tracks. Lifting her gaze to the trees around them, she frowned when she saw several that appeared to be dead, which was why there were so many needles carpeting the ground.

Disease? Lack of water? She wasn't sure.

Quickening her pace, she caught up to Shane and Bryce. They were moving faster now. The dog apparently was on a mission, sniffing intently as he trotted through the brush. Thinking back to the shallow cave they'd left behind, she realized that while the search was continuing, she'd know next to nothing about her grandfather's disappearance if not for Shane and his K9, Bryce.

Reinforcing the incredibly valuable service the Sullivan family provided to the community.

They walked in silence for several minutes. The image of the zip tie flashed in her mind. It wasn't easy to focus on the positive when she had no idea how these guys were treating her grandfather. If they wanted something from him—what she no idea—it made sense that they'd give him food and water at the very least.

When Shane signaled for a break, she let out a sigh of relief. She walked around town to stay in shape, but this was a whole new level of hiking. Maybe she needed to rethink her exercise plan.

"Down, Bryce," Shane said. The dog lowered himself to the ground, his tongue lolling to the side as he panted. The expression made Bryce appear to be smiling.

"How much farther?" she asked as Shane handed her a bottle of water from the pack.

He shrugged. "I think we'll run into the clearing soon. I was hoping this guy had spent time elsewhere, but Bryce is heading toward the clearing."

She took a long drink of water before handing the bottle back. "I was afraid of that."

"Me too." Shane drank from the water bottle, too, then poured the rest into the collapsible bowl for Bryce. "I was hoping this guy had other hiding spots in the woods. But it seems as if he stayed at the cave last night so that he would be close enough to try to sneak into the cabin."

She nodded. "That makes sense."

"Except for what he's looking for in the cabin." He sighed. "I'm starting to think we need to tear the place apart."

"I already searched the place, Shane. I didn't find anything that would explain this." She waved a hand at the woods around them. "Certainly nothing that justifies why anyone would go as far as to kidnap my grandfather."

"This guy has come back twice that we're aware of." Shane held her gaze. "His attempt to get inside early this morning indicates we're missing something."

She wanted to argue, but he had a point about the guy coming back to the cabin on two separate occasions, most recently in the middle of the night. Possibly wearing night-vision goggles to enable him to see clearly.

Maybe the guy had gone back while they'd been driving around searching for the four-wheeler trailer. She hadn't noticed anything out of place inside the cabin, but that doesn't mean someone hadn't been inside to look.

"Okay, fine. We'll go back and look again." She sighed. "It doesn't make sense that Grandpa would have hidden something like this from me."

"You mentioned not seeing the photos and newspaper clippings in the box you found in his closet," Shane reminded her. "I know you said your grandfather was adopted as a young boy, but maybe he knows more about his real parents than he told you."

"Maybe, but I don't see how his elderly parents could

possibly pose a threat." She shook her head. "No, I'm not buying that. I'm more inclined to think this is a case of mistaken identity. That these guys who took Grandpa think he's someone he's not."

Shane shrugged without saying anything more. She sensed he didn't agree with her. Then she remembered the sister she'd uncovered. A woman who would be her great-aunt. "I think we should go back to that DNA report. Maybe this is related to my grandpa's sister. Or her kids." The more she turned that idea over in her mind, the more she glommed onto it.

Maybe this was about simple greed. It could be that her grandpa's sister or her family believed they deserved the cabin and ten acres of land.

And if that was the case, she'd gladly hand it over in exchange for getting her grandfather back safe and unharmed.

SHANE WASN'T CONVINCED the DNA report was related to Marvin's kidnapping, but he was ready to head back to the cabin. He still felt like searching the place was their best chance at finding something helpful.

He rose to his feet and set the bowl of water near Bryce. "Are you ready to work?"

Bryce eagerly jumped to his feet and eagerly lapped at the water. When Shane offered the scent bag, he barely sniffed the strip of denim. Shane had wondered if Bryce's alert at the cave was for the bad guy's scent or Marvin's.

Likely both. Bryce was smart enough to keep the two scents separate in his mind.

"Search! Search for Bad Guy." Shane tucked the

collapsible bowl back into his pack as Bryce lowered his nose and set off on the trail.

Consulting his compass, he estimated they'd reach the clearing in about ten to fifteen minutes. Following Bryce up and around the rock outcropping to the cabin had taken them at least a mile or two outside their normal search area. But from the clearing, he could easily find his way back to Marvin's cabin.

As he followed Bryce through the trees, he pulled out his phone. Like yesterday, there was no service in the area. He made a mental note to touch base with Deputy Paul Holland. They'd left well before the deputy would have been on duty.

If the police hadn't found the truck or trailer, then they were pretty much back to square one. Which led him right back to his idea of searching the cabin.

Bryce made an abrupt turn to the east. With a frown, Shane adjusted his course. "Search Bad Guy," he called encouragingly.

The dog kept going at a brisk pace. Shane rested his hand on the butt of his weapon, ready for anything. They were making more than enough noise that the bad guy could easily hear them coming.

And he could very well be hiding nearby.

Yet he felt certain Bryce would growl in warning the way he had earlier this morning. Still, he didn't like risking his dog. Or Libby.

Once more, he found himself leaning on prayer in a way he hadn't for several years. *Dear Lord, keep us all safe in Your care!*

His heart lodged in his throat when he lost sight of his dog. He leaped over a fallen log, then breathed a sigh of relief when he saw Bryce sniffing something on the ground. Then his dog turned, sat, and let out a sharp bark.

"Good boy!" Shane carefully scanned the area but didn't see anyone hiding nearby. He glanced back to make sure Libby was coming, then approached the location where Bryce alerted.

There was nothing obvious on the ground. With a frown, he wondered what had caught Bryce's attention enough for an alert.

A dark crimson stain on a leaf caught his gaze. He knelt to get a better look. Then he saw another drop of reddish brown a foot away.

Blood? He frowned, glancing at Bryce. His K9 sat straight and tall, his dark eyes boring into Shane as he waited for his reward.

"Good boy!" He pulled the ducky out and tossed it. "Good boy, Bryce."

"What did he find?" Libby asked.

He hesitated, then remembered his promise to keep her informed. He gestured to the leaf. "Looks like a small amount of blood."

"Grandpa's blood?" Her face paled.

"No, I believe it belongs to our bad guy." Shane pulled the scent bag containing the scrap of denim from the pack and lifted it for a closer look. "There's a little bit of blood on this piece of denim fabric, too, see?" He handed it to her. "I think Bryce got a piece of him when he tried to take him down."

"Then he really is a good boy." Libby nodded in satisfaction.

"For sure. Interestingly, I don't remember seeing any blood in the cave." Shane turned to scan the area. "Could be our perp didn't stop to examine his wound until he reached this location."

"Maybe his leg wound will get infected!" Libby winced, then added, "I shouldn't have sounded so excited about that. What I mean is, if the dog bite is bad enough to need antibiotics, the police might be able to grab him at the hospital."

"Good point." He pulled his phone out again. Still no service. But he used the device to take pictures of the leaves with blood on them. Maybe the deputies would be interested in seeing them. "We can't call anyone yet. Let's keep pushing forward. The sooner we put the sheriff's department on notice about that possibility of this guy needing medical attention for a dog bite, the better."

"Great." Libby looked relieved to have another plan other than searching the cabin. He wasn't sure why she was so resistant to that idea. "Bryce really is amazing that he was able to find the scent here."

"For sure, he's amazing." Shane would praise his dog any day. "Come, Bryce."

The shepherd trotted over and regurgitated the yellow ducky into Shane's hand.

"Good boy." He gave the dog a good rub. He decided against telling Bryce to search for the bad guy. The guy may have taken a different route down the mountain. Yet chances were good that Bryce would simply lead them to the road, the way he had yesterday. Knowing their bad guy had been injured, Shane figured it was more important to get in touch with the police. "Let's go."

Bryce sniffed the air with interest but didn't resist as Shane turned back in the direction of the clearing.

Ten minutes later, the path widened into the clearing. Bryce sniffed the ground, then sat and let out a sharp bark.

"You've already alerted here." Shane frowned, eyeing his dog. "And I didn't tell you to search."

Bryce simply sat staring at him expectantly. The best dog stare came from Maya's dog, Zion, but Bryce was a close second. Shane debated for a moment, then decided it was best to keep the dog engaged. He dug the ducky from the front pocket of his pack and tossed it into the air. Bryce jumped up as if he hadn't seen the ducky in hours rather having been rewarded a few minutes ago. "Fine, but hurry up and celebrate. We need to keep going."

Libby grinned. "You're such a softy when it comes to Bryce."

Didn't he know it. With a grimace, he nodded. "Yeah, well, it's all about the search game. I need him to be excited to win." He shook his head at how Bryce ran around with the ducky in his mouth. "Let's go. Bryce will catch up."

Shane double-checked his compass again before taking the lead. Thankfully, he had a good sense of direction, even back when Chase was teaching them how to avoid getting lost during night searches.

And it was easy to see the path they'd taken twice the day before.

When they reached the halfway point, his phone vibrated. He stopped and turned to pull the device from his pocket. There were several text messages from Joel and Alexis. "We have cell service."

"Do you want me to call the deputy?" Libby reached for her phone too.

"Yes, please do." He scrolled to his recent calls and found Alexis's number. Taking a few steps away from Libby who was already speaking to the sheriff's department, he called his sister.

"Hi, Shane," Alexis greeted him. "We've been waiting to

hear from you. Do you have another search expedition in mind?"

"Not yet." He glanced at Libby, then gave his sister the abbreviated version of recent events, hitting the high points of Bryce taking off after the guy and coming back with a strip from his jeans. And the blood they'd found on the trail. "We're heading back to the cabin now. We're hoping this guy seeks treatment for his dog bite."

"Good for Bryce," Alexis agreed. "Joel wanted you to know we're hanging around the ranch in case you need us. Maya and Chase left bright and early for a search and rescue mission in Jackson; two groups of tourists got split up in the mountains. Don't worry, Maya promised to be care-ful," Alexis added. Shane knew his sister was referring to Maya being four months pregnant. "Because of the recent calls, we've put the ongoing search for our parents' plane recovery on hold for a while. Trevor and his K9, Archie, are working a missing hiker northwest of Cody, and Justin has his K9, Stone, in Yellowstone. As you know, Jessica and Logan are still on their honeymoon, so that means you have me, Joel, and Kendra if needed."

As the baby of the family, Kendra tended to be used in search and rescue missions as a last resort. Not that she wasn't smart and capable. Her K9, Smoky, was a great tracker. It was partially because they sought to protect her. Especially after Kendra had taken a bad fall in November of last year.

Still, he also knew that keeping Kendra out of the search would hurt his sister's feelings. "Thanks, but I think we're good for now." He didn't want to waste his family resources in the height of tourist season. Summer was the easiest time for them to search for their parents' plane or any of the remains from the crash, but it was also when their search and rescue services were needed the most. Having several searches going on throughout the state wasn't unusual. "I appreciate you and the others sticking around the ranch for a while, though. If things change, I'll reach out. And if you get a call out, let us know too."

"Sounds good. Later." Alexis disconnected from the call.

"I spoke with the sheriff's department dispatcher." Libby crossed over to join him. "She agreed to get the message to all local hospitals to be aware of a guy with a dog bite on his ankle or lower leg and to call the police if he shows up seeking treatment. However, she also warned me not to get my hopes up because a patient presenting with a dog bite wasn't an automatic report to the police."

"That's true. The only automatic reports are knife and gunshot wounds. But maybe the doc will be worried about a dog bite enough to make a call to the authorities." He eyed his watch. They'd set out with Bryce at six thirty, and it was barely eight fifteen now. How much of a head start did this guy have on them? Hopefully not too long. "If they can put the hospitals on alert, we still stand a good chance of getting him in custody. By the time he made it off the mountain to reach the road and his vehicle, the closest hospital is at least sixty to seventy miles away. And even then, with it being tourist season, there's a good chance he might have to wait for a while to be seen."

"I hope you're right about that." She didn't look encouraged. "I keep thinking if he's smart, he'll choose to hit an urgent care clinic. If that's the case, he could have walked in and already be out by now."

"Hey, where's that positive attitude I've come to appreciate?" he asked with a half smile. "We know more now than we did when we headed out. Especially the part where Bryce left teeth marks on the guy."

"Yes, that's true." She managed to smile back. "I'm grateful for everything you and Bryce have done for me and my grandfather." She tilted her head to the side, regarding him thoughtfully for a long moment. "You know, Shane, you should smile more often. You look very handsome."

He twisted his expression into an exaggerated smile that felt more like a grimace. "Like this?"

She threw back her head and laughed. "No, now you look like a crazed maniac who chases people through the woods with an axe."

Since that was his intent, he smiled for real. Her comment about his looks shouldn't have mattered, but it did. Strangely, he enjoyed spending time with Libby. Even with the seriousness of her grandfather's disappearance, her cheeriness was rubbing off on him.

Something he never would have thought possible.

The memory of her quick kiss on his cheek made the back of his neck grow hot. He'd liked that, too, a little too much. He had chosen this career of search and rescue. Libby didn't owe him anything.

"We should keep going." Now that they'd come this far, he was anxious to get back to the cabin. "Bryce, come!"

The dog bounded toward him, dropping the rubber ducky into his outstretched hand. Bryce was well trained compared to Chase's Rocky who would drop the toy on the ground rather than handing it to Chase.

"Good boy." He stuffed the ducky away and hurried down the trail. He glanced at Libby. "Paul hasn't reached out with an update?"

"No, but I mentioned that to the dispatcher too. About how I'd like an update on the investigation," she clarified. "She promised someone would get back to me."

He nodded without expressing his concern that in this

situation, no news was not a good thing. Okay, maybe it was a relief that they hadn't discovered Marvin's dead body tossed along the side of the road, but it seemed to him that the police were no closer to locating Libby's grandfather than they were.

"I'm sure we'll hear from Paul soon." He forced himself to sound positive.

She shrugged. As they rounded a cluster of aspen trees, her expression brightened. "I can see Grandpa's cabin from here."

"Great." He was glad to know they were close. He glanced over to where Bryce was nosing the aspen trees with interest. "Come, Bryce."

The dog immediately trotted over, his tail swooshing from side to side. As they emerged from the woods to cross the grassy area of the backyard, Bryce abruptly began to growl.

"Stop, Libby." He halted in his tracks, his hand going to his gun. "You better stay here with Bryce while I check it out."

"Wait, take Bryce with you," Libby urged. "I don't want you facing off with this guy alone."

Unwilling to put her or his dog in harm's way, he shook his head. "Stay back." Before she could mount another argument, he broke into a run. His goal was to cross the open area as quickly as possible.

When he reached the back side of the house without anyone shooting at him, he considered his mission to be a success. Taking a deep breath, he edged toward the patio doors. Then he ducked back when he realized one of them was open a half inch or so.

Hadn't Libby locked them? He couldn't remember.

Holding his weapon ready in his right hand, he reached

out to open the patio door with the other. Then he quickly stepped over the threshold. The interior of the cabin looked about the same. The blanket Bryce used for a bed was still on the floor, and the pillow and blanket he'd left on the sofa were still there.

Shane quickly moved through the house, making sure nobody was hiding there. He was about to head outside to check the cellar when he noticed something was different.

The box of pictures and newsletter clippings Libby had left on the kitchen table was gone.

Someone had come inside for the sole purpose of taking it.

9

———

Waiting with Bryce was agonizing, especially when Shane disappeared inside. She found herself staring at the cellar doors, half expecting someone to come bolting out from there.

But the exterior of her grandfather's cabin remained quiet and still.

Finally, Shane emerged from the house. He lifted a hand, indicating she should stay back, before heading toward the cellar. He lifted the door and descended the stairs, holding his weapon ready.

After what seemed like an eternity, he climbed back out. "Come, Bryce!"

The dog had seemed content sitting beside her, but now he raced across the open field to reach Shane's side. She followed more slowly.

"Good boy." Shane knelt and stroked the dog's fur. "You're a good boy."

"Why did he growl?" She frowned, looking around curiously. "Doesn't appear that anyone has been here."

"The bad guy was here." Shane rose to his feet and led the way back inside the cabin. "Notice anything missing?"

Her gaze landed on the kitchen table. "The box of photos and newspaper clippings." She stared in shock. "That makes no sense. Why on earth would the bad guy have come back here to take them?"

"I was hoping you could tell me." Shane slid his weapon into his belt holster. "Did you notice anything specific about them?"

Her chest squeezed painfully. She wished now that she'd taken the time to go through the contents before leaving. But really, how was she to know the bad guys would come back to steal it? "Not really."

"Think, Libby." Shane took a step toward her, his blue gaze boring into hers. "Something must have caught your eye."

"Everything in the box caught my eye!" She dragged her fingers through her hair, doing her best to maintain some semblance of control. "I remember thinking the photograph sitting on the top of the pile was of my grandfather with two other men." She envisioned the picture in her mind but couldn't recall seeing a date along the edges of the photo. "Maybe close to fifty years ago? When Grandpa was nineteen or twenty years old?"

"That's a good start." Shane took her hand and drew her toward a kitchen chair. "Take your time. Can you remember anything else?"

Why hadn't she gone through the entire box? Why? She drew in a deep, calming breath, closed her eyes, and tried to envision the newspaper article. There wasn't a full headline because the paper had been folded in half. The ink had faded over time. Something about large. No, wait, there were two words. At Large.

She opened her eyes. "The ending of the headline was something about 'At Large.' No clue what the rest of it was."

"Did a date catch your eye?" Shane pressed.

"No. Although with the photograph on top being fifty or so years ago, it might be from a similar time frame." She shook her head, feeling helpless. "I can't believe the bad guy came back just to steal the box."

"Did you lock the patio doors behind us?"

She frowned, sighed, and shook her head. "No. I should have, but I was hoping Grandpa would get free of his captors and make his way back here. I wanted him to be able to get back inside."

"That's understandable," Shane said, although she could tell he wasn't thrilled at the news.

"Grandpa rarely locks his doors, and honestly, I don't even know where he keeps his keys. It's never been an issue as nobody bothers him way out here." She winced, then added, "Well, until now."

"That's okay. I guess it's a good thing they didn't have to break in." Shane reached over to take both of her hands in his. "I'm not blaming you. I'm just trying to figure out what happened."

Ridiculous tears pricked her eyes. Grumpy Shane was trying to cheer her up. She tightened her grip on his hands, wishing she never had to let him go. "Thank you."

"For what?" He looked adorably confused. "I didn't do anything."

"Oh, Shane." She offered a watery smile. "You're sweet."

"O—kay." He still looked uncertain.

She leaned in to kiss his cheek. He turned his head, and for a moment, their mouths were only an inch apart. When Libby understood he wasn't going to close the gap, she did.

Their kiss was brief but intense. As she sat back, she

strove to breathe normally. "I, uh, maybe you're right about searching the place. I mean, the fact that this guy was in the cellar, then came back to steal the box makes me think there might be something important hidden on the property."

"Yeah." His low, husky voice made her shiver. The burning intensity of his gaze made her long to throw herself into his arms. But she managed to stay in her seat. "I think that's a good idea."

Tension simmered between them. Libby had to force herself to pull her hands from his. She rose, leaning on the kitchen table as her weak knees threatened to buckle.

She gave herself a mental shake. It wasn't as if she'd never kissed a man before. So why this weird awareness of Shane?

Turning away, she nearly tripped over Bryce who was stretched out on the floor. The poor dog scrambled to his feet, looking up at her in confusion.

"Sorry." She lightly patted the dog's head not even feeling foolish for talking to him as if he could understand her. "I didn't see you there."

"He's fine." The corner of Shane's mouth quirked in a half smile. "I have to say, I'm glad you're not afraid of him anymore."

"He's a good boy. I've learned I can trust him not to bite me." She still found the large dog intimidating.

"Where should we start?" Shane asked.

She glanced wryly around the small cabin. "I'm sure this won't take very long. I'll search Grandpa's room, maybe there's another box of old photos in there. Maybe you should double-check the cellar."

"That works." Shane stood. "Come, Bryce."

She turned and headed back to her grandfather's bedroom. Like earlier, when she'd been looking for a handgun, she felt bad about violating his privacy. It nagged at her that Grandpa had never shown her the old photos or newspaper clippings. Even when she'd mentioned wanting to do a DNA sample to see if they could find his biological family.

She paused in the middle of the room, remembering how unenthusiastic her grandpa had been about the DNA testing. At the time, she'd chalked his reluctance up to being uninterested in change. Grandpa didn't travel, didn't really go much beyond his property here and the occasional visits to Cody, mostly for doctor's appointments. He never wanted to travel outside the state, claiming everything he loved was here, so there was no reason to leave.

Now she wondered if there was a deeper reason Grandpa didn't want to poke into the past. Especially after the way he'd stared in shock at seeing the DNA report where she'd identified his sister.

The picture she'd glimpsed had featured her grandfather with two other men. Not a woman. But it occurred to her now that maybe there was a picture of his sister in the box. Maybe even a photograph of the two of them together.

As kids? Grandpa had said he'd been adopted as a baby. The DNA testing didn't reveal if his sister was older or younger. They hadn't gotten that far in the process.

It hurt to know that Grandpa had kept things from her. The contents of the box, certainly, and maybe even more.

Did he know the guys who'd taken him?

She sighed and headed toward the closest bedside table. This one had a worn paperback novel and a few scraps of paper that were meaningless to her. Nothing else. She headed over to the other drawer, which was empty. She frowned, vaguely wondering where the Bible was that she'd given him.

Maybe in the living room? She'd check later.

Turning, she started in on the closet next. She eyed her grandfather's shirts, verifying that the red plaid shirt was missing. The bit of thread stuck to the fallen log where Bryce had alerted the very first time must have been from his clothing. She blinked back the threat of tears, refusing to believe the worst.

They were going to find him very soon.

She pushed the clothes aside and found a second box tucked away in the corner. This one was on the floor, not up on the shelf overhead where a couple of cowboy hats sat.

Her pulse surged as she reached for the box. It was light, which made her frown.

She carried it to the bed and opened the flaps. The box was light because there were about two dozen photographs inside. When she picked up the top one, she smiled when she saw herself astride a bike, her red hair pulled back into two pigtails on either side of her face.

Shuffling through the rest of the photos, she realized they were all of her and her mother. None of Grandpa, which was strange.

And why had he kept these pictures of her separate from the other box? It wasn't as if either box was too full to accommodate additional items.

Leaving that box on the bed, she continued her search. But she didn't find anything else. Not in the closet, under the bed, or anywhere else in the house.

Whatever the bad guys wanted wasn't hidden inside the cabin.

And as she stared out at the open land, she found herself wondering if her grandfather had buried it somewhere on the ten acres of land surrounding them.

THE CELLAR WAS A BUST. Not that he'd really expected to find a hidden doorway or anything obvious. Still, he had to assume the bad guy had come down here for a reason.

He slapped his hands on his jeans to get rid of the dirt and dust. He had told Bryce to guard the top of the cellar doorway. As he turned to climb out of the cellar, Bryce jumped to his feet, looking expectant.

His dog was happier when he was working. Shane closed the cellar door with a loud thud, then took a moment to give Bryce some attention.

"Are you a good boy? Huh?" He ran his fingers over the shepherd's soft pelt. "Don't worry, we'll be back at it soon."

Bryce wagged his tail, glancing over when Libby stepped out of the cabin. From the dejected expression in her eyes, he figured her search had been unsuccessful too.

"I don't suppose Bryce can search for buried treasure."

He arched a brow. "No, sorry. The only buried items our dogs tend to find are bullets, shell casings, or in the case of Alexis's dog, Denali, the remains of dead people." He hesitated. "You don't want me to have Alexis and Denali search the property, do you?"

"No." She pursed her lips as she scanned the area. "I don't think there's a dead body out here. That wouldn't be a reason to kidnap my grandfather. But I'm starting to think my grandfather buried something of value on his land." She sighed. "It's strange, though, since I know he doesn't spend much money. So why on earth would someone want to find whatever it is that he's hidden?"

"That's a good question." He didn't know Marvin Tolliver very well. But based on the stark yet neat cabin, the older man certainly wasn't living beyond his means.

"I don't know where to go from here." Libby frowned. "I

want to keep searching for Grandpa, but I don't know where to start."

"I know." A sudden thought occurred to him. "We could try doing an online search for newspaper headlines that end with the words At Large."

"From fifty years ago?" She made a face. "I don't know about that."

He wasn't well versed on searching for newspaper articles from fifty years ago either. "I should call my brother-in-law Doug Bridges. He might know how to access information from fifty years ago."

"That's fine, but what can we do in the meantime?" Libby was clearly frustrated. "Go back into the woods to track the bad guy's scent?"

He was hesitant to keep pushing Bryce on what would likely be a fruitless mission. But she was right in that sitting around wasn't going to help.

Before he could say anything, Bryce's ears pricked forward, and the dog began to bark. Libby startled badly, but he caught the low rumble of a car engine.

"Stay here. Come, Bryce." He gave his K9 the hand signal to heel and moved quickly around the house. A white and black sheriff's deputy vehicle was rumbling up the long driveway.

He relaxed and told Bryce to be quiet. Then he called, "Libby? Looks like Deputy Paul Holland is here."

"Why didn't he call?" She ran around the corner of the house to join him. Then she grabbed his arm in a tight grip. "Bad news? They always give bad news in person."

"Don't, Libby." He covered her hand with his. "Maybe he's just checking in."

She watched the approaching squad with apprehension. The vehicle stopped a few feet behind his K9 SUV.

Then she visibly relaxed when Paul slid out from behind the wheel, raising a hand in greeting. "Libby, Shane. I heard from dispatch that you had an intruder here last night?"

"We did, yes." He offered what he hoped was a reassuring smile to Libby. "Come inside and we'll fill you in."

"Okay." Paul gave Bryce a wide berth.

"You don't have an update?" Libby asked as they headed inside. "I take it there's been no sign of my grandfather?"

"I'm afraid not." Now Paul looked somber. "I traced the license plate to a vehicle owned by a man named Ward Engler. He's a local resident living in a house nearby. By the time one of our deputies arrived at the property, there were no four-wheelers on the trailer. Since we had no reason to suspect him of wrongdoing, we let it go."

Shane suppressed a sigh. "I guess I can understand that. Did you verify if he had a grandson?"

"No, that's not exactly an easy task. The kid could have a different last name." Paul shrugged. "We focused on keeping an eye out for trucks pulling trailers. Unfortunately, we didn't see any others." When Shane frowned, Paul added somewhat defensively, "I know what you're thinking, but we patrol a large county."

Shane glanced at Bryce who now had the scent of at least one of the bad guys imprinted on his brain. If they ran across the truck now, he wondered if his K9 would alert. Especially if Ward Engler was friends with the younger bad guy.

Still, there wasn't anything more they could do on that front. Driving aimlessly around again searching for a truck and trailer was not a good use of their time.

"What's this about someone showing up here?" Paul asked, changing the subject.

Shane nodded. "I was asleep on the sofa when Bryce

growled a warning. I noticed movement outside the patio doors." He gestured to them. "I rushed over and gave Bryce the command to get him. The guy had a head start." He bent over his backpack to pull the plastic bag out containing the strip of denim. "Bryce got a piece of him, though. He brought this back to me."

"How did the guy get away?" Paul frowned as he examined the fragment of cloth. "Wouldn't be easy to shake a hundred-pound dog loose."

"I heard an engine. I'm sure he was on the four-wheeler and gunned it." Shane could imagine Bryce planting his front paws to hold the guy back only to fall back when the strip ripped free. "Look at it closely. I think there's blood on there."

"Blood?" Paul smoothed the plastic to see better. "There is a dark stain there, but it could be dirt or grime too."

"I had Bryce follow the bad guy's scent," Shane explained. "He led us to a shallow cave near an outcropping of rock. That's where we found this." He pulled the plastic piece of a zip tie that had been in the cave. "To be fair, Bryce could have been alerting on either Marvin's scent or the bad guy's. Not sure. But as Bryce continued tracking this guy, he alerted in a clearing where we found blood stains."

"Blood stains?" Paul glanced at his dog. "He can smell blood?"

"He can smell anything that leaves a specific scent behind. Sweat typically works better." Shane pulled out his phone and brought up the pictures. "I didn't bring the evidence back with me, but you can see that those stains appear to be blood."

"This is why you're thinking the guy may be heading to a hospital?" Paul looked skeptical as he handed the phone back to him. "It's not like he lost a pint of blood or anything."

"No, but the wound could get infected," Libby said.

"Dog bites are notorious for that," Shane said in agreement. "I'd actually be more surprised if his wound didn't get infected."

Paul sighed. "I don't know. It's not much to go on."

"Why not?" Libby looked upset. "What can it hurt to question someone who comes in for treatment of what appears to be a dog bite? I can't imagine patients walk into the hospital with that type of injury every day."

"Not a dog bite, but other wild animals maybe." Paul spread his hands. "If this guy is operating on the wrong side of the law, he's more likely to claim he was bitten by a fox or a coyote than admit a well-trained K9 tried to take him down."

Shane hated to admit that Paul had a point. "I still think any male presenting with an animal bite to his lower leg should be considered a suspect."

"It's not exactly probable cause," Paul drawled. "We can ask questions, but that's about it."

"That should be enough. Questions about where the injury happened and having a name would be helpful too." Libby appeared annoyed with Paul's logical approach to this issue. "If the guy has a criminal record, that may give you probable cause for an arrest."

Paul didn't say anything for a long moment. "We have put the alert out to all hospitals and clinics in the area. So far, nobody has reported anything matching our request for information."

"There's still time," Libby insisted. "It takes a while for an infection to set in."

"You're a medical expert now?" Paul sounded testy.

"My work at the hospital is in billing, so no." She bit her lower lip in a way that reminded Shane of their brief but sizzling kiss. "But I don't think it happens in an instant."

"She's right. It takes a few hours for an infection to set in." Shane gave her a reassuring smile. "I've learned enough first aid through the many search and rescue missions we've carried out. The ones who suffer the most are those who have been lying in the woods with an exposed injury for more than twenty-four hours."

Libby flashed a grateful smile. "I appreciate your insight, Shane. It makes sense to me that infections take time."

Paul picked up the plastic zip tie. "You think these guys tied your grandfather up with these?"

"Yes, I do." Libby leaned forward. "Please, Deputy, you really need to help find him. He's going to be seventy in a few months, and I'm so worried about his health. He doesn't deserve to be treated like this."

"I promise we're looking for him," Paul said. Although Shane did not sense a strong level of confidence from the deputy. "I'll let the others know about the blood and reinforce the plan of checking hospitals and clinics."

Bryce nudged his leg. "Maybe include veterinary clinics," he advised. "This guy could try a roundabout way to get antibiotics."

"I can do that." Paul stood and moved across the room to speak softly into his radio. Shane couldn't hear exactly what he was saying, but he hoped the right message was getting across to the rest of the local police.

Maybe he should call his brother-in-law Doug. Maya's husband was a federal agent now for the DEA, so a missing person was well outside Doug's jurisdiction. Yet at the same time, Shane was losing hope that the locals could pull this off.

Not that he'd confide his concerns to Libby.

"Okay, we've included the earlier alert to include veterinary offices," Paul said, coming back to the kitchen table. "Shane, send me those cell phone pictures."

"Of course." He used his phone to send the photos. It took a few minutes because Marvin's cabin wasn't wired for the internet.

It wasn't unusual for people of Marvin's generation to live off-grid. Yet it struck him now just how isolated Libby's grandfather was. And that, according to Libby, Marvin preferred it that way.

Because he had something to hide? The words *At Large* flashed in his mind.

Escaped Prisoners At Large?

Burglars At Large?

Or worse, Murderer At Large?

He didn't want to believe any of those things and knew Libby would be upset if he even mentioned the possibility. But the idea wouldn't leave him alone.

"Anything else?" Paul glanced between the two of them.

"Not that I can think of." Shane noticed the hopeful expression in Libby's brown eyes dimmed. "We're going to keep searching the woods, though. See if we can come up with anything new."

"Sounds good." Paul edged toward the door. "Please keep us in the loop."

"Always." Shane glanced at Libby, who was staring down at the floor.

He walked Paul to the door. "Call us as soon as you find anything," he said in a low voice, "even if it's bad news."

"I will." Paul gave him a nod, then strode to his squad.

Shane turned to see Libby's face buried in her hands.

Bryce crossed over to nudge Libby's legs. She let out a hiccuping sob.

"Libby, please, don't." He quickly went over to put a comforting arm around her shoulders. "We're going to find him."

"Are we?" Her muffled voice tore through him.

"Yes, we are." He crouched beside her, searching for something to say. "We'll head out again soon, okay?"

"Thank you." She sniffled loudly and lifted her head. "I need a tissue."

He found a box in the living room and quickly brought it over. She blew her nose and wiped her eyes. "Will you pray with me?"

"Uh, sure." He couldn't say no. She stood and wrapped her arms around his waist. Surprised by the hug, it took half a second for him to wrap his arms around her too.

"Lord Jesus, please keep my grandfather safe in Your care," she whispered. "And we also ask that You continue to guide us as we seek the truth. Amen."

"Amen." Shane couldn't remember the last time he'd prayed with someone that wasn't his family.

Yet doing so with Libby felt right. In a way, that was both comforting and scary at the same time.

10

———

"Thanks, Shane." Libby would have loved to stay nestled against Shane's chest forever, but obviously, they needed to do something, anything to find her grandfather. Drawing a deep breath, she lifted her head and started to step back.

Shane didn't release her. Instead, his mesmerizing blue gaze clung to hers. His voice was low and rough when he spoke. "I haven't prayed like that in a long time."

"Was that because of Rebecca?"

"Yes, that and losing my parents." He cleared his throat. "My family has always attended church and prayed. So I was taught to believe from an early age. But it's hard to keep that faith alive after suffering so much loss."

"That's true." She tried to smile. "It wasn't easy for me after losing my mother. It's the knowing she's in a better place that offers comfort."

"Yes, that does help." The corner of his mouth kicked up in a semblance of a smile. "And we've often talked about how good it is that our parents were together. We miss them, of course, but they had each other at the end." His smile faded. "I only hope their death was quick and painless."

She wasn't familiar with the details of the plane crash that had taken his parents' lives. Or Rebecca's car crash either. "I'm sure they held on to each other until the end."

He nodded. "Imagining them together like that helps." He paused, then abruptly added, "I was supposed to be with Rebecca that night."

She caught her breath. "You were?"

"Yeah. But I got hung up with a group at the dude ranch." His gaze darkened. "I was doing a favor for my parents, taking a rich group of city slickers out on a ride. Supposedly they all had riding experience, but they came across as rookies to me. One of the women fell off her horse and broke her ankle. I had to place a splint, and our ride back to the ranch was slow." He shook his head. "There wasn't much I could do, stuff happens. But I remember Rebecca was upset with me about breaking our date. The next morning, her car was found at the bottom of a ravine. She died even though the airbags had deployed. The local sheriff's deputy concluded that she'd swerved to avoid an elk or some other animal that likely had wandered out into the road. The truth is that if I had been there as promised, she'd still be alive today."

Her heart ached for him. "I'm so sorry, Shane." She didn't necessarily agree with his conclusion, maybe things would have been different. Or maybe they would both have died that night.

He shrugged and looked away. "I've been told God has a plan for us, but sometimes it's hard to understand why people have to die so young. Like why should that have to be a part of some master plan?"

"I don't know. Keep in mind God doesn't promise that

we'll never hurt or suffer while here on earth." She tightened her grip around his waist. "God does promise us that if we believe in Him and accept Jesus as our savior, we will have everlasting life. That's what really matters."

He gathered her close in a tight hug, then released her. "Thanks, that helps. For now, it's time for us to come up with a plan of our own. One related to finding your grandfather."

She nodded. "I think we need to go back to Cody so I can get my laptop computer. Maybe if we can search on that headline from all those years ago, we'll gain some insight as to who might have taken Grandpa."

He grimaced. "I like that idea, but you need to be prepared for what we might find."

"Prepared how?" She frowned. "What are you talking about?"

After a moment's hesitation, he drew her to the living room sofa. Bryce jumped up to follow them, stretching out on the floor beside Shane. *His shadow*, she thought with a smile. The dog would clearly do anything for Shane. "Sit down for a minute, okay?" She did, and Shane dropped down next to her. "You mentioned the last two words on the headline you glimpsed were 'At Large,' right?"

"Yes. I remember seeing those words very clearly." She wished again that she'd have taken a closer look the moment she'd found the box. Now it was gone, and she was afraid her grandfather would never get it back.

"I believe the headline might be referring to escaped criminals being at large," Shane said, breaking into her thoughts. "Or maybe it's that the suspects are at large."

Suspects? She was glad she was sitting down. "No, I'm sure the headline wasn't referring to my grandfather."

"Then why did he keep it hidden away for so long?"

She shook her head, her mind whirling. There was no

way her grandfather could be involved in something criminal. The man she loved was a sweet, kind, and wonderful man. He'd doted on her, and they'd gotten close since her mother's passing. "I don't know. Maybe it's something else. Something painful that he didn't want to tell me about because it makes him sad."

"I'm not saying your grandfather did anything wrong," Shane hastened to reassure her. "Maybe he witnessed something he shouldn't have. Or maybe there's another explanation, bad memories as you suggested. I'm not sure what we'll find, but I do think you need to be prepared in case . . ." He hesitated, then added, "In case you don't like what we uncover."

Hard to argue his point. Especially since it seemed as if her grandfather hadn't bothered to show her any of the photos or articles in the box. Why would he keep something like that a secret? Especially the photographs? And why would that secret cause someone to come after him now, all these years later?

Realization dawned, and she wanted to kick herself for being so stupid. "The DNA report."

"What about it?"

She stared at Shane, feeling sick to her stomach. Her grandfather's disappearance was likely her fault. "I believe these guys tracked my grandfather here because I submitted his DNA into the system. Grandpa may have been staying off-grid on purpose—until I put him out there in the spotlight for these jerks to find."

"We don't know that's how your grandfather was found," Shane protested.

"How else?" She threw her arm out to encompass the cabin. "Grandpa has been living here for the past forty years. As far as I know, nobody has ever come looking for him, until now!"

"Forty years?" Shane looked surprised. "Way out here in the middle of nowhere? How did he support himself?"

"He lived off the land, hunting and fishing primarily. He worked in construction in the early years when my mother was growing up. I mostly remember him as doing guide work for a local outfitting company." She frowned, trying to remember the name. "I think it was called O'Grady's Hunting Outfitters or something like that. They were super busy in the spring and fall obviously. I remember as a kid I didn't get to see Grandpa as much during those times of the year. But in summertime, I spent weeks here at the cabin while my mom worked." Those were some of the best memories of her life.

"What about your grandmother?" Shane asked.

"She died when my mom was young. I never knew her." She'd always wondered why her grandfather hadn't remarried. "Her name was Lydia."

"I'm sorry for your grandfather's loss. But this is the first I've heard of this guy O'Grady. Did you ever meet him?" Shane asked. "I take it that's his last name. Do you remember his first name?"

"His name was Michael O'Grady. I met him years ago, but I haven't seen him recently. Not since Grandpa retired from doing guide work, which was probably six years ago or so?" She abruptly jumped off the sofa, unable to sit still. Bryce lifted his head, watching her with his intense dark eyes.

She didn't pay much attention to the dog, her thoughts spinning. What if Shane was right about the criminal aspect of that headline? What if her grandfather had witnessed something or, worse, participated in something illegal all those years ago? Now that the possibility was out there, she was desperate to find the truth. "We need that computer."

"Okay, we'll drive back to Cody." Shane rose to his feet. "Or we can stop in Greybull and buy a laptop."

"Why on earth would I buy one if I have one at home?" She frowned, annoyed. "That's wasteful."

"Well, tell me this, does Greybull have a library? It's closer, and we can use the computer there if needed." He glanced down at Bryce. "I'm just thinking it's better to stay close to the cabin, just in case your grandfather can return. Or if we hear from Paul or the sheriff's department related to our perp and his dog bite. Going all the way to Cody and back will take a big chunk of our day."

"You're right. There is a library in Greybull. When I was a kid, I would participate in their young adult book clubs during the summer." She smiled at the memory. "I like the idea of sticking close. Oh, and I'll leave Grandpa a note." She went around Bryce to find paper and a pencil. "I hope you're right about his being able to get here. I'd like nothing more than to come back here to find Grandpa waiting for us."

"Me too." Shane shouldered his backpack. "Let's go."

Her note was brief. *Grandpa, I'll be back soon. Love, Libby.*

As she followed Shane back outside to his specially designed K9 SUV, she prayed this trip to the library would help them learn something crucial about the men who'd taken her grandfather.

And more importantly? Figure out a way to get him back safely.

SHANE OPENED the back hatch for Bryce. His K9 gracefully leaped inside the crate area. Bryce didn't mind riding in the back, but he could tell his dog would rather be back on the scent trail.

Something he'd like too.

"Soon, boy," he promised, then closed the hatch. He slid in behind the wheel, glancing at Libby. She was staring off in the distance, clearly lost in thought.

He couldn't blame her for being concerned about what they'd find. The more he thought about it, the more he suspected that this was a secret Marvin had never planned to reveal to Libby.

Until his past had come back to haunt him.

"We should keep an eye out for a truck and trailer," Libby murmured as he headed toward the highway. "Maybe we'll catch a glimpse of these guys."

"Sure." He doubted these guys were still driving around with Marvin in the back seat. He felt certain they were holding him someplace close by.

Logically, he knew they could be anywhere. Yet one of them must not be too far away considering how he kept showing up at Marvin's place to search for, what exactly? He had no idea. But he found it interesting the bad guy had taken the box of photos and newspaper clippings with him.

Maybe because the contents inside the box might incriminate him?

He found himself hoping that was the case because right now, they were fresh out of leads and ideas of where to search next. He had confidence in Bryce's ability to find Marvin and the bad guy he'd chased, but narrowing down to a specific location would be helpful.

As he drove to Greybull, Shane kept a wary eye on the

rearview mirror. Not so much looking for a truck pulling a trailer, but more to make sure they weren't being followed.

So far, so good.

"I want to thank you again for everything you're doing to help me find Grandpa," Libby said.

"I don't mind. This is what we're trained to do. Besides" —he paused and waited for her to look over at him—"I have a vested interest in this too. You and your grandfather matter to me. I am not leaving until we find him."

"That's very sweet, Shane." Her smile was sad. "I pray we find him very soon."

He nodded and focused on driving. He couldn't imagine why he'd confided in her about the circumstances around Rebecca's death. Oddly, since spending time with Libby, he hadn't given his life with Rebecca much consideration.

Until Libby had asked him to pray with her.

Maybe she was right that it wasn't up to him to question God's plan. His life had changed dramatically since losing his parents, and if he were honest, he couldn't say for sure if his relationship with Rebecca would have lasted. He'd cared about her, hoped to someday marry her, but he'd been young back then.

He was older and wiser now. And being with Libby was a reminder of what he could have if he was willing to open his heart to love again.

The trip to Greybull didn't take that long. Warm summer weather meant the town was teeming with people. Most were likely tourists, but he knew the locals would also be outside, taking advantage of the bright sunshine and mild temperatures.

Winters in Wyoming were long, cold, and hard.

"I think the library is right here along the main highway." Libby leaned forward in her seat. "I remember it being a single-story building . . . there! That's it. Turn here!"

He pressed on the brake and pulled into the parking lot. He opened the back hatch for Bryce, then killed the engine. "I hope these people aren't too strict on the no dog rule."

She grimaced. "I hope not too."

Shane went around to get Bryce. The dog was still wearing his K9 vest, which might help. Just in case, he grabbed a leash. Bryce wasn't a fan of the thing, but he would tolerate it if needed. "Be on your best behavior, okay?"

Bryce wagged his tail as if to say *Aren't I always?*

Libby led the way inside, clearly familiar with the place. Shane gave Bryce the command to heel, and the dog fell into step beside him. A woman behind the main checkout counter frowned when they walked in. But then she noticed the Sullivan ranch logo on Bryce's vest, and her expression softened.

To his surprise, she didn't comment on Bryce being there but quickly returned to her computer screen as if pretending she never saw them.

Fine by him.

Libby was already seated at one of the two computers. The other one housed an older woman who used one finger to type something into the screen.

"Lie down," he told Bryce as he stood behind Libby. The dog stretched out on the floor, resting his head between his front paws. "Good boy," he praised.

The older woman never looked over, and he wondered if she might be hard of hearing.

"Let's see," Libby murmured as she nimbly entered a series of search commands. He was surprised to see she entered the phrase: Suspects at large in case from 1975 to 1985.

The hits were numerous. He was surprised at how many cold-case murders were listed on the screen. He leaned forward. "Maybe you need to narrow the type of suspect. Murder versus robbery, that kind of thing."

She glanced at him, then nodded. When she started with murder suspects, the links that popped up on the screen were mostly related to serial killers and old cold-case murders that had been solved using new and improved DNA testing. Libby's shoulders were tense as she scrolled through the various sites.

"This could take a while," she said with a sigh. "I'm not sure why I thought this would be easy."

He shared her concern. He didn't want to be there all day either. "Maybe enter unsolved cases where suspects are at large from that same time frame?"

She tried that, and again, murders were at the top of the list. She began opening the links one by one.

Bryce lifted his head and stared up at Shane. He didn't bark or whine, but Shane belatedly realized the dog needed to go out. "I'll be back in a few. Come, Bryce."

The dog shot to his feet and trotted alongside him as they headed outside. Shane found a grassy area off to the side of the library building. He didn't have to tell Bryce to get busy, the dog was sniffing the area with interest and then made a circle before deciding on the right spot to squat.

Shaking his head with amusement, he belatedly realized he'd left his baggies in the backpack. As soon as Bryce was finished, he headed to the SUV to grab them.

A large black truck rolled past the library. Shane frowned, thinking it looked similar to the one they saw yesterday, the one pulling a trailer. The vehicle moved too fast for him to get a good look at the license plate, though. Still, he pulled out his phone and looked at the picture.

Yep, same make and model. Then again, trucks were as common out here as elk roamed the forest. Without a license plate, or a good look at the driver, he couldn't provide a positive ID.

He quickly cleaned up after Bryce. What did Paul Holland say the guy's name was? Ward something. Eaton?

No, Engler. Ward Engler.

He was tempted to drive through town to check the guy's license plate, despite the fact that Paul claimed the deputies had already crossed him off the list. What if Bryce alerted on the guy this time around?

It was worth a shot.

He sent Libby a text message as he opened the back hatch of the SUV. *Running a quick errand. Will be back soon. S.*

She responded with an okay sign.

Convinced Libby would be safe enough in the public library, he closed the hatch and quickly ran around to get into the driver's seat. He backed up and pulled out onto the highway. He'd noticed the driver of the truck had taken a right-hand turn at the intersection, so he mirrored his movements.

Driving slowly, he scanned the area for the truck. He should have asked Paul for Ward Engle's address. Did he even live in Greybull?

Or was this where the bad guys were keeping Marvin Tolliver?

Not the latter, he quickly decided. Small towns were notorious for gossips. Keeping an old man hidden away would likely draw unwanted attention.

Still, that didn't mean Engler wasn't involved. He hit the phone button on his dashboard. "Call Paul Holland."

A moment later, the call was connected. Unfortunately, Paul didn't pick up, forcing Shane to leave a message. "Paul, it's Shane. I'd like to know where Ward Engler lives; you mentioned he's a local resident. I just saw him in Greybull and was curious if this is where your deputies talked to him. Call me." He ended the call, trying not to feel guilty over the white lie. He didn't know for sure the guy driving the black truck was Engler.

He drove all the way through Greybull without running across the black truck. Was he making a big deal out of nothing?

Probably. At the far west side of town, he turned around and headed back toward the library. He was halfway back when the back end of a black truck caught his eye. He hit the brake, wincing as the car behind him came to a quick stop, too, then turned into the parking lot.

The lot was packed with cars, including a large black truck. He drove past it, checking the rear plate to see if it matched the one he'd taken a picture of.

It was!

The only empty parking spot was way off in the back. Shane quickly pulled in and released the back. He'd take Bryce inside and see if the dog alerted on Bad Guy's scent.

A long shot? Maybe. But it was better than doing nothing.

Grabbing his pack, he poured some water into a bowl for Bryce. The dog lapped at it, then stared up at him expectantly. He loved knowing Bryce was eager to get to work.

"This is Bad Guy." He offered Bryce the scent bag. "Search! Search for Bad Guy!"

Bryce sniffed the scrap of denim, then wheeled and lowered his head to sniff the parking lot. Shane stayed back, giving Bryce room to roam. K9s loved to please their handlers, so it was important to make sure he didn't lead Bryce to a forgone conclusion in any way.

He wanted Bryce to alert only if the bad guy had left his scent anywhere near the black truck. If not, that was fine too.

Although he'd already decided to take Bryce inside the restaurant to have him sniff around Ward Engler. That may prove more useful than hoping the guy had been in or around the truck.

Bryce moved all around the parking lot but never alerted. When his K9 went past the black truck, he sighed.

Of course, it couldn't be that easy.

"Search," he called encouragingly. "Search Bad Guy."

Bryce made a complete loop of the parking lot, coming back to stand near Shane. He bent and ran his fingers over the dog's fur. "You're a good boy. We're going to try one more thing, okay? Come."

He stood and walked to the main entrance. Before he opened the door, he repeated the command in a low voice. "Search Bad Guy."

The restaurant was packed. Shane stood for a moment, trying to spot the man he'd run into the previous evening. Those who were facing him didn't look familiar, but several people sat with their backs facing the door. Bryce was sniffed with interest at the people sitting closest to the door.

Shane didn't see a single empty table, and from the harried expressions of the two servers, it appeared they were so busy it wouldn't pay to stick around if there was one available. His stomach rumbled with hunger at the scent of bacon, burgers, and fries.

A movement toward the back of the restaurant caught his eye. Bryce hadn't alerted, but Shane quickly moved through the restaurant. He saw an empty seat at the old-fashioned counter along with a half-empty plate of food and cash left behind.

Had Ward Engler taken off?

Shane headed toward what he now realized was a rear entrance. He pushed open the door but didn't see anything at first.

Then the black truck backed out of the parking spot and drove away.

"Bryce!" He turned to go back inside. His K9 was sniffing near the empty stool but still didn't alert.

He frowned, wondering if he was on the wrong track. But if so, why had Ward Engler taken off so fast?

Most people in these parts didn't waste food.

"Come, Bryce." He headed outside using the same back exit. Maybe he could follow Engler.

Bryce trotted beside him, still sniffing. He winced. "It's okay, Bryce. Stand down."

The dog looked disappointed.

As he opened the back hatch, his phone rang. Expecting Paul, he was surprised to see Libby's name on the screen. "Hi, Libby."

"Shane?" Her voice sounded choked as if she'd been crying. "I think I found it."

His gut clenched as he slammed the hatch and hurried to get behind the wheel. "What did you find?"

"An unsolved Colorado bank robbery from forty-eight years ago." She sniffled loudly. "One of the robbers was killed at the scene, along with a local police officer. Another man was arrested, but the third man got away."

He could easily imagine the headline "Bank Robbery Suspect At Large." He started the car and backed out of the space. "Does it mention your grandfather by name?"

"No." She sniffed loudly again. "It says that a man

wearing a face mask suspected to be a Wellington Fox Security truck driver by the name of Maxwell Tucker was the one who got away with the cash. I—I think that's my grandfather."

Oh yeah. He thought so too.

11

Still reeling from what she'd uncovered, Libby printed the article. The library requested a fee to mitigate the cost of the paper and ink, and thankfully, she had a spare couple of dollars in her pocket.

There wasn't a single doubt in her mind that Maxwell Tucker was her grandfather. He'd used the same initials for his new name, likely because it was easier to remember. Her stomach twisted painfully; she hated the thought of her grandpa being involved in something illegal.

The picture she'd glimpsed of him standing with two other men flashed in her mind. Had those two men been his accomplices? She picked up the article from the printer. Off to the side of the main picture featuring a truck that had been abandoned on the side of the road, there was a small, grainy photo of her grandfather. He looked so young; she imagined it had been his driver's license photo.

As much as she'd wanted to know the truth about what had happened to her grandfather, this was more than she'd bargained for. One man dead, one arrested and the other at large. Not to mention a police officer who was killed.

How on earth had her grandfather escaped? She swallowed hard and headed outside. She was still staring down at the article when Shane pulled up in front of the library. He lowered the passenger-side window. "Get in, Libby. We should head back to the cabin."

Dazed, she nodded and reached for the door handle. Yet as she slid inside, she realized she didn't want to go back to the cabin. "We need to go back inside and see what we can find out about these two men who were accomplices. Harry Stern and Greg Olson."

Shane frowned. "I think we need to turn those names over to the local police. They have the resources to find them."

"We can't do that, Shane. I'm afraid they'll arrest Grandpa." Maybe that was what her grandfather deserved, but she couldn't bear the thought him spending time behind bars. She held his gaze, hers pleading for him to understand. "I think we should try to find them by ourselves first. Considering we have Bryce, we just need a starting point."

Shane sighed. "And then what, tell them to hand your grandfather over? I think it's obvious they're looking for the money that was never recovered."

Knowing her grandfather had taken the cash made her wince. "We don't know what he did with the money. Maybe he turned it in? Or left it someplace?" Even as the comments tumbled from her mouth, she knew that wasn't likely. In truth, she couldn't help but wonder if her grandfather had already spent the money. Maybe that's how he's supported himself and his family all these years.

But if that was the case, then why had these guys kidnapped him? No, the more she thought about how frugally her grandfather lived, the more she believed he hadn't spent the money. "Can Bryce find buried cash?"

"Not unless it's buried with guns and ammo. And that also depends on how deep it was placed in the earth."

She tried not to show her disappointment. "We can't just give him money to sniff and tell him to search?"

"No. It doesn't work that way." Shane held her gaze. "Libby, we've looked through your grandfather's cabin, including the cellar. Twice. I don't think he hid the money someplace obvious like under the bed. And he likely wrapped the cash in something, then stuffed it inside a metal box to preserve it." He shook his head. "Bryce is good, but that's asking a lot."

"Okay, so we need to figure out some other way to find the cash." Then she winced. "What am I saying? I don't care about the cash, we need to find my grandfather."

"Why don't we call Deputy Paul Holland?" Shane's reasonable tone irrationally made her mad. "He can find them quickly."

"No." She stared down at the article in her hand for another long moment, then pushed open her car door and jumped out. "I'm going to spend some time searching on the computer. You can do whatever you like." Without waiting for him to answer, she slammed the car door and hurried back inside the library.

The computer she'd been using earlier was still free, so she quickly dropped into the chair. She double-checked the article and verified that Greg Olson was the man who'd died. Harry Stern was the one who'd gone to jail.

She started with Harry first, wondering if the man had recently gotten out of prison. Maybe Harry had spent his time behind bars, stewing over the way Maxwell a.k.a. Marvin had gotten away with the cash. Easy to imagine the guy making it his sole mission to come after her grandfather for his share. She went back to the original search to look for follow-up articles on Harry Stern's time in jail.

After a few minutes, she found an article mentioning that Harry Stern had been released from prison after serving fifteen years, having gotten out earlier than the original sentence of twenty years for good behavior. She wondered if the authorities had been able to prove Stern hadn't killed the police officer. Had her grandfather? She hoped and prayed he hadn't.

Yet it was clear Harry Stern had been out of jail for a long time. Her stomach knotted again as she realized that putting her grandfather's DNA into the system must have given Harry the clue he'd needed to find him.

Instead of helping her grandpa find his family, she'd led his coconspirator straight to him.

Then she realized that the whole adoption story was probably a lie. A cover to make up for the bank robbery. Tears burned her eyes. *How many other lies, Grandpa?* she thought wearily. *How many?*

Libby pulled herself together with an effort. The lies, her grandfather's past—none of that was important now. She needed to find him. And that meant learning more about Harry Stern.

Unfortunately, Harry didn't have much of a presence online. Likely because he'd spent such a long time in jail. Which begged the question of how a man who'd lived for years behind bars had figured out how to look for her grandfather using DNA sites?

He probably had help from someone of a younger generation. Much the way she was searching for information right now. Doing the math, she considered Harry must have gone to prison at the age of twenty. Not impossible for him to have kids of his own, but she leaned toward his getting help from a niece or nephew.

When she felt someone come up behind her, she startled. Then she had to smile when she felt Bryce's wet nose pressing against her arm.

"What can I do to help?" Shane's voice was quiet.

Stupid tears pricked her eyes again. The fact that he'd come back in to support her was sweet, but she was already hitting brick walls. She glanced up at him over her shoulder. "Nothing much for you to do. I haven't found much on Harry Stern; he's the guy who was captured and sent to jail back when the robbery took place. He only served fifteen years, so he's been out for a while now."

Shane nodded. "You're thinking the DNA led Harry and his cohorts to your grandfather."

It hurt to hear him state the truth so bluntly. "Yes. I'm responsible."

"You didn't rob the truck," Shane said softly.

"I know." She stared blindly at the computer screen for a long moment. "It's hard to believe Grandpa was involved in this."

"I'm sure he has regrets," Shane murmured. "He may have buried the cash specifically because it was blood money."

He was just saying that to make her feel better, and it worked. "I hope you're right about that. Grandpa isn't a hard or ruthless man. I'm sure he felt terrible after the way things went down all those years ago. Especially after the officer was killed."

"Forty-eight years is a long time to keep a secret of this magnitude," Shane said thoughtfully.

She wanted to hug him for being so nice about the fact

that the man she loved had committed a terrible crime. Forty-eight years ago, sure, but still a crime.

That thought gave her pause. What was the statute of limitations on a robbery? Probably not forty-eight years.

Then again, one man had died in the robbery along with a police officer. And there was no statute of limitations on murder.

A dull headache settled at the base of her skull, and nausea churned in her stomach. She went back to the article, searching for the answer as to who may have shot Greg Olson or the cop who'd died.

But there was nothing specific.

She dropped her head into her hands, her thoughts whirling. Maybe they did need to turn this over to Deputy Paul Holland. Finding her grandpa alive was worth the risk.

"Hey, it's okay." Shane gently cupped her shoulders in his big, strong hands. "Don't stress. We'll figure something out."

She lifted her head and looked up at him. "You were right, Shane. We need to call Paul about this."

He nodded and released her. "I'm sorry. I know that puts your grandfather's past in the spotlight."

"Yes, in a big way. But I don't want my grandfather to die over this either." She pushed herself to her feet, nearly tripping over Bryce who'd stretched out on the floor beside her. Maybe the dog had sensed her distress. The German shepherd was big and fierce looking, but he was a softy at heart. "Let's go call him."

"Why don't we have him meet us for lunch?" Shane raked a critical gaze over her. "You should eat. We need to stay strong in case we get a lead on your grandfather's whereabouts." The corner of his mouth kicked up in a rare smile. "You know how Bryce can be when he's hot on the scent."

She wasn't sure food would stay down, but Shane was right about the need to stay strong. Bryce could move much faster through the wooded terrain than she could, so she managed a nod. "Okay. Lunch works for me."

"Great. We'll find a place here in Greybull. I think the Four Corners Café isn't too far." He stepped back, and added, "Come, Bryce."

The dog jumped up to stand at his side. Then he lowered his front end in a long stretch, before returning to all fours and wagging his tail.

"He's a good boy." She smiled at the dog as they made their way out of the library. There was something about the K9 that lifted her spirits. At least a little.

She folded the article into fours and slipped it into her pocket, wishing she could tuck the truth away as easily.

Her heart felt heavy as they headed to the Sunshine Café. Yet even as she listened to Shane making the call to Paul about having new information related to her grandfather's disappearance, she couldn't help but pray there was a way out of this.

That somehow they'd rescue her grandpa while finding a way to avoid his having to spend the rest of his life in jail.

Tension radiated off Libby in waves. She was approaching this upcoming meeting with Paul with trepidation and resolve.

He wished he could make this easier for her. He missed her sunshine-and-roses attitude toward life.

After parking at the Sunshine Café, he released the back

hatch so Bryce could jump down. The SUV was designed to start up automatically if the interior of the car got too hot, but he didn't want to take the risk.

Besides, this meeting with Paul could take a while.

"I'm glad you're bringing Bryce inside," Libby said as he held the door open for her. "I like having him close by."

"You do?" Her statement surprised him. "You're not afraid of him anymore?"

"No." She shrugged, and added, "Although that could change if he came charging at me with his teeth bared."

"That won't happen," he assured her. "He only charges after bad guys or those he perceives to be a threat."

"I know. I've seen him in action." She glanced around the café. "There's one booth open, let's grab it."

He followed her to the table. Several people looked at Bryce curiously, but when the dog curled up beneath the table, he was soon forgotten.

"I'm not sure I can eat." Libby put a hand over her stomach, frowning at the menu on the table before her.

"Please, Libby." He ached to hold her. "I know it's difficult, but your grandfather needs you, needs us to find him."

"That's the only thing keeping me going." She sighed and gave the menu a push. "I'll try the chicken sandwich."

"Sounds good." He caught their server's eye. A woman old enough to be his mother hurried over. Her name tag identified her as Cynthia.

"What can I get you to drink?" Cynthia asked.

"Iced tea for me." Shane cocked a brow. "Libby?"

"Iced tea is fine, and I'll have the chicken sandwich with fries. Thanks." Libby's attempt at a smile was pathetic.

"Cheeseburger and fries for me." Shane glanced past Libby at the door. "We have someone joining us, but he won't be here for a while."

"That's fine." Cynthia didn't appear fazed by the addition. She picked up the menus and headed over to get their iced teas.

Libby took a sip of her tea, then pulled a folded paper from her pocket. "Here, you should read this before Paul gets here."

He gulped his tea and pulled the paper close. The article headline wasn't a surprise; Libby had already given it to him. But as he read the article that had outlined how three men had robbed a Wellington Fox Security truck transporting over two million dollars in funds from one bank to another, he understood why she'd been hit so hard by the story.

Her grandfather had been the driver of the Wellington Fox Security truck. A job he'd held for over a year. And that meant he was most likely the one who'd come up with the robbery plan.

Especially since Marvin Tolliver was the only one who'd gotten away with the cash. Leaving one man dead along with a police officer and the third man to be picked up by the FBI a day or two later.

No wonder Libby looked as if she wanted to throw up.

"Grisly reading, huh?" She looked so dejected. "I never would have believed Grandpa was capable of such a thing."

"Forty-eight years ago," he gently reminded. "He was young and had probably gotten carried away by the idea of having so much money."

"By stealing from others?" She shook her head. "No way. He'd know stealing was a sin."

"Lots of people sin, and your grandfather may not have been a believer back then." He was determined to give the guy the benefit of the doubt. "Besides, it's how he's lived since that time that matters."

"Does it?" She grimaced. "I'd like to think so. But I have a feeling Paul is going to pull the FBI in on this."

He knew that was true. There was one FBI agent in Wyoming, located in Cheyenne. Shane had met Special Agent Griff Flannery on previous cases. Griff was a decent guy, roughly his age. Some feds were hung up on their fancy title, but Griff was more interested in getting the job done. "Try not to worry."

She nodded without saying anything more. Their meals arrived shortly afterward.

Libby didn't mention saying grace, so he decided to take the initiative. "Dear Lord Jesus, we ask You to keep Marvin safe in Your care. Please continue to guide us as we seek the truth. And please bless this food we are about to eat. Amen."

"Amen," Libby whispered. Then she lifted her gaze to his. "Thank you, Shane."

"Of course." In the back of his mind, Shane knew he was treading on dangerous ground, willing to do just about anything to make Libby happy.

And oddly, the prayer had come naturally.

Maybe he had absorbed some of this sibling's faith over the years. He added a special prayer for God to grant Libby the strength she'd need to get through this, before digging into his cheeseburger.

The food was good, although Libby only ate about half of her chicken sandwich along with a handful of fries. They were just finishing when Paul walked in.

"Are you hungry?" Shane asked as Paul slid into the booth beside him. Beneath the table, Bryce shifted and let out a heavy sigh as if he'd been hoping they were going to work soon. He reached beneath the table to smooth a hand over his K9's fur. The dog settled down, resting his head on Shane's feet.

"Nah, I grabbed something earlier." The deputy swung his gaze between Shane and Libby. "What's this about new information?"

Libby looked sick as she pushed the article toward Paul. "Read this and tell me what you think."

Paul picked up the printout of the article and quickly scanned it. Then he frowned and read it again more slowly. Paul looked up and pinned Libby with an incredulous gaze. "Your grandfather is the infamous Maxwell Tucker?"

"Yeah." Libby took a sip of her barely touched iced tea. "At least, that's our theory. To be honest, it's the only one that makes any sense."

Paul's wide gaze swung toward Shane. "You agree?"

"Hard not to. Someone broke into the house to search the place more than once." He gestured to the article. "Now we know what they were looking for."

"I need to call the FBI," Paul said, his expression grim. "An armored truck robbery from Colorado, even one that took place so many years ago, is way outside my jurisdiction."

"I get that, but it's going to take Griff time to get here from Cheyenne. Even if he comes by plane, that will take several hours, maybe more. What about doing some legwork in the meantime?" Shane tapped the article. "Consider what we know so far. Harry Stern only did fifteen years of the twenty ordered by the court. It stands to reason that he's been harboring a grudge against Maxwell Tucker a.k.a. Marvin Tolliver for a very long time."

"Too long maybe," Paul said thoughtfully. "Why come after him now? And how did he find Marvin in the first place? From what I can tell the guy—er, Libby's grandfather —has been living off-grid for a long time."

"That's true," Libby said softly. "That is until I decided to submit a DNA swab to find my grandpa's birth family. He told me he was adopted, and I thought he'd like to know if he had siblings, aunts, uncles, cousins . . ." Her voice trailed off.

"Libby believes that entering her grandfather's DNA into the database is how Harry Stern found him. And set out to kidnap him, searching for the fortune that Stern missed out on after being arrested."

Paul didn't look convinced. "I doubt it's that easy."

"Probably not, since Harry Stern would be roughly the same age as Marvin, sixty-nine or even seventy by now," Shane agreed. "But look at what Libby has accomplished in her brief time searching for information. Harry Stern went to jail when he was only twenty years old, in an era where computers were not as common as they are now. But he could easily have nephews or other relatives helping him out."

"That's true." Paul appeared to warm to the idea. He picked up the article again and read it for a third time. It didn't take long for him to nod in agreement. "Okay, I think you guys are onto something."

Before Shane could ask about their next steps, Libby's eyes widened. "Wait, could this be the guy we saw with the trailer? What was his name? Ward something?" She narrowed her gaze, then added, "Yes, I remember, it's Engler. Ward Engler." She tapped the article. "Maybe Ward is a nickname because he was on a prison ward." Her gaze darted to his. "Didn't you say you saw his truck here in town?"

"I did." Shane's pulse kicked up as he remembered how the guy had bolted out of the restaurant when he and Bryce had come inside. He turned to face Paul. "After I dropped Libby off at the library, I caught a glimpse of a black truck. It was outside a diner, and I asked Bryce to search."

"Bryce?" Paul frowned. "Why?"

"I was hoping that if your guy Ward Engler was involved with the kidnapping, and he'd spent time with the bad guy Bryce had chased, my K9 might alert on his scent." He didn't add that it was a long shot in this case. "He didn't alert outside, but the license plate of the truck parked in the lot matched the one Libby and I saw yesterday. The one owned by Ward Engler."

Paul shot him a pained look. "I hope you didn't accuse the guy of being a criminal."

"I didn't get a chance," Shane said. "When I brought Bryce inside the diner, Engler bolted out the back, leaving a half plate of food behind."

"That's weird," Paul agreed.

"He must be guilty of something," Libby said. "Otherwise, why get up and leave like that?"

"That's what I thought, too, but he was gone before I could give chase." He held Libby's gaze. "And that's when you called about finding the article."

"Okay, hold on," Paul protested. "A guy leaving a restaurant doesn't equate to guilt."

"Maybe not, but it's not exactly the act of an innocent man either." Shane picked up the article and quickly scanned it. "There's no picture of Harry Stern here, but you can get one, can't you? One from the files back then so that we can compare it to the man we know now?" When Paul hesitated, he added, "Come on, Paul. Libby's grandfather has been missing for more than twenty-four hours. We're on a time crunch here. There's no reason we can't keep working the case while waiting for Griff."

"Okay, okay. But I need to make that call to Griff. He'll

want in on this for sure and will also have to coordinate with the feds from Colorado too. I'll be back in a few." Paul rose and left to head outside where he could talk without being overheard.

Shane reached across the table to take Libby's hand. "This is the right thing to do."

"I know." Her expression was sad. "I just feel bad for Grandpa. None of this would have happened if I hadn't done that stupid DNA test."

"He'll be okay." Shane squeezed her hand. "Nobody can carry a secret like this with them forever, Libby. For all you know, it's been eating at him for a long time now. Trust God. We just need to have faith that everything will work out okay in the end."

She managed a weak smile. "You're being awfully optimistic for a man who expects the worst."

"This is the new me," he teased. "I've turned over a new leaf. This is the cheerful, optimistic Shane."

Her husky laugh sent a warmth rushing through him, and it was all he could do not to jump across the booth to pull her into his arms.

Oh yeah, this was dangerous ground all right. Steps toward something he'd avoided for years.

And if he were honest, he had no interest in looking for a way out. Quite the opposite.

When this was over, he didn't want to let Libby go.

12

───────

"Thanks, Shane." Libby tugged her hand from his and scooted out of the booth. "Excuse me."

She ducked into the restroom, used the facilities, then stared at her reflection in the mirror for a long moment. As touching as it was for Shane to try cheering her up, she knew that once they found her grandfather, the local police or the FBI would arrest him.

Hopefully, they'd arrest the kidnappers too.

She turned away, tunneling her fingers through her hair. This entire situation was surreal. Why on earth had her grandfather decided to rob the armored truck in the first place? The man she'd known for the past thirty years had never been greedy. He'd seemed happy and content with his simple life.

And she couldn't help but wonder if he'd kept the money all this time or slowly spent a little here and there to avoid detection. The federal government had a way to track the serial numbers on stolen money, so it seemed unusual that her grandpa could have avoided being caught if he'd used the cash.

Yet what was the point of taking the money if you weren't going to use it?

So many questions without answers.

She headed back out to the table. Shane stood as she approached, his blue eyes searching hers. "Are you okay?"

"Yes." She wasn't, but there was no point in belaboring the point. She slid back into the booth and stared at her half-eaten sandwich. Maybe she should take the rest back to the cabin. If—no, *when* her grandpa came back home, he might be hungry.

"It's going to work out," Shane said in a low voice.

She managed a nod.

"Okay, Griff is on his way," Paul announced as he returned to the table. He looked relieved to have the feds involved. "But you're right that it's going to take him at least seven hours or more to drive here. He doesn't want to fly because he wants his own vehicle."

"That's understandable," Shane said. "I'm glad he's coming. Now I think you should see if you can find an early photograph of Ward Engler and match that with our suspect, Harry Stern. Maybe Engler isn't his real name. They could be one and the same."

"You watch too many movies," Paul grumbled. He remained standing near their table. "It's not as easy to use a fake ID as you think."

"Yet we know now that Grandpa was able to accomplish that very thing," she pointed out. "And for nearly fifty years." She had no idea how her grandfather had managed that feat but tried to stay focused. "I agree with Shane. Ward Engler deserves some intense scrutiny. Especially after the way he took off leaving half his meal behind when Shane and Bryce showed up at the café."

"I'll work on that angle." Paul eyed them somberly. "I'd

like you to head back to Libby's grandfather's cabin. That way I'll know where to find you if I learn anything new." He stepped back, then glanced at Bryce who was lying beneath the table. "We'll likely need your K9 to assist with the search."

"I'd like nothing more than to use Bryce to help find Marvin." Shane pulled cash from his wallet for the bill. "I'll take Libby back to the cabin. But please keep us in the loop."

"Will do." Paul nodded, then turned and left.

Libby leaned forward. "I think we should see if we can find Ward Engler ourselves."

"We can't do that. It's not safe." Shane left cash on the table, then slid out of the seat. "Come, Bryce."

The large shepherd crawled out from beneath the table and eagerly followed Shane to the door. Libby hastened to keep up. Shane paused and held the door for her. She waited until they were striding toward the SUV before saying, "Drop me off at the library again. I'll search for more information about Harry Stern. There's probably an article somewhere that mentions him getting out of jail."

Shane sighed. "I have a better idea. We'll buy a laptop and use my phone as a hot spot so we can use it at your grandfather's cabin."

"That's a waste of money," she began, but he waved her off.

"I consider it an investment. I could use a new laptop anyway. We passed a computer repair store. I'm sure they have new and refurbished laptops available." He opened the back hatch for Bryce, then reached for the passenger-side door. "We'll be more comfortable at the cabin."

Watching as Bryce jumped into the back, she realized he was concerned about his dog more than anything. She relented with a nod. It was his money to waste, and for all she knew, he really did need a new computer. "Okay, that's fine."

A moment later, they were back on the road driving through town. She kept her eyes peeled for the black truck, but she didn't see it. She didn't have confidence in Deputy Paul's ability to dig into the possibility of Harry Stern being Ward Engler. She wasn't an expert at searching either, but she had found the article about her grandfather. Stood to reason she might be able to dig up info on Engler.

The computer repair store was bigger than she'd expected. The guy who sat behind the main counter gave Bryce a wary look but didn't complain. Smart move as Shane headed straight for the new computers set up along one wall.

She checked out the used machines and was impressed at the selection. She made a mental note to check back here if she needed to replace her current laptop, as the prices were reasonable.

Yet she wasn't surprised Shane chose a brand-new top-of-the-line computer, the most expensive of the bunch.

"Hey, it's a good price," he said when she arched a brow.

Maybe so, but it still seemed extravagant. The Sullivan K9 Search and Rescue Ranch must be doing better than she realized. How, when they only accepted dog food as payment for services, she had no clue.

His problem, not hers. Once Shane had tucked the new laptop beneath his arm, they headed outside. Bryce trotted alongside, sniffing the air with interest.

"It's amazing he doesn't get distracted while doing searches." She opened her car door as Bryce jumped into the back crate area.

"He's well trained and likes to play the search game."

Shane closed the back and went around to tuck the new laptop on the floor of the back seat. "I'll work with him while you work on the computer. He needs to burn off some energy anyway."

"Good idea." That would be better than having Shane hovering over her shoulder to watch her work. Libby knew she was growing too attached to him. This forced togetherness wasn't real. Once they both went back to their regular lives, she wouldn't see him again.

Especially if she had to visit her grandfather in jail. The thought made her wince. Would he be taken to a large federal prison far away from Cody? She had no idea where the various penitentiaries were located.

The thought of seeing her grandfather on a limited basis while he was behind bars was depressing. She did her best to shake it off. First, they had to figure out who kidnapped her grandfather and get him back.

Then she'd worry about the repercussions of her grandfather's actions.

The drive back to the cabin didn't take long. Shane pulled into the driveway and stopped the vehicle. He put a hand on her arm when she reached for the door handle.

"Not so fast. Bryce and I need to check the place out first." He pushed a button on the key fob to open the back hatch for Bryce. "Once it's clear, we'll let you know."

Since the kidnappers had been there before on more than one occasion, she didn't argue. In fact, she found herself holding her breath as Bryce trotted forward, sweeping his nose from side to side as he took in the scents.

When Bryce began to growl low in his throat, Shane reached for his weapon, and shouted, "Come out with your hands up where I can see them!"

She watched the front door of the cabin intently, but

nobody emerged. Bryce's growling grew louder, then he let out a couple of short barks.

"Last warning," Shane called. "Don't make me sic my dog on you."

Still no movement from the cabin. But then she heard an engine roar to life. Without thinking it through, she scrambled from the car as Shane and Bryce bolted around to the back.

"Stop!" Shane shouted. "Get him, Bryce! Get him!"

Her heart was in her throat as she rounded the cabin in time to see a man disappearing on a mini bike into the woods. Her first thought was that he wasn't riding a four-wheeler as they'd thought.

Her second thought was to be afraid for Bryce as he barreled into the woods after the intruder. What if the bad guy shot him?

Shane must have had the same concern, because he called out, "Stop, Bryce! Come!"

A long thirty seconds later, the large shepherd emerged from the woods. Shane ran forward, dropping to his knees to examine the dog.

"Is he okay?" she asked breathlessly.

"Yeah." Shane took a minute to hug the animal, then stood. "I don't like the way the bad guys keep showing up here. I don't think we should stay."

She was torn by indecision. If her grandfather was able to get away, he'd come straight here.

But Shane had a point about the bad guys showing up every time they left the place. The fact that they returned to the cabin so often made her realize they wouldn't stop until they'd found the money.

And worse, once they had what they wanted, they'd likely kill her grandfather.

"Come on, Libby." Shane frowned when he noticed she was staring blindly out into the woods where the bad guy had vanished. "You need to pack a bag."

"I'm not leaving." She finally turned to look at him. "Did you notice he was on a minibike? Not a four-wheeler?"

"Yes." He had been surprised by that, although he shouldn't have been. These guys seemed to have a variety of vehicles at their disposal. "The engine sounds higher than a typical four-wheeler."

"He's staying somewhere close by," Libby said with a frown. "Maybe even close enough to watch us. To take advantage of the moment we leave to come back to search for the missing money."

"That's possible," he admitted. "But it doesn't change the fact that we aren't safe here."

"I can't leave." She rounded on him, her eyes flashing with temper. "Don't you get it? If they find the money, they'll kill him. If we stay close, they're less likely to come back."

Or they'd come back with guns to take them out of the picture, for good. But the new determined-to-be-optimistic version of Shane couldn't bring himself to point that out. Instead, he considered their options. "Let's get inside the house. I'll call my siblings." He belatedly remembered several of them were out on other searches, leaving limited resources behind. "I'm sure Joel and Alexis won't mind helping again."

Libby gave a jerky nod and turned to step around him. He caught her arm again. "Me first, with Bryce. Stay behind me."

She didn't argue. As he walked toward the patio doors, he noticed the cellar door had been left open. This was where the bad guy had been when they'd arrived. Not in the house, but in the cellar.

Bryce trotted alongside him. He growled low in his throat, sat at the top of the steps, and let out a sharp bark.

"Good boy!" He tossed the rubber ducky in the air for Bryce as a reward for alerting on the bad guy's scent. Obviously, he was the same one Bryce had chased earlier.

So much for thinking the guy would be forced to seek treatment for his dog bite.

He pulled his weapon and slowly took the stairs down into the cellar. This time, he stopped abruptly when he noticed there was a large hole along the back of the wall. And the shovel that had been used to make it was lying inside the opening.

He knelt to peer inside. The hole appeared to be at least three feet in height and maybe four feet in depth. Just enough room for a man to crawl inside.

He stared at the hole for a long moment. Marvin Tolliver must have told his kidnappers that he'd buried the stolen money in the cellar. He couldn't imagine they'd go to the effort of digging without knowing where to start.

What he didn't know was if Marvin was being honest or if Libby's grandfather was giving them a fake destination to buy time.

His gut leaned toward the buying-time theory. Yet the cellar was a good place to bury stolen cash.

Backing away from the hole, he stood, then abruptly turned to stare at the shovel. He reached for his phone to call Paul. The deputy answered on the first ring.

"One of the bad guys took off when we arrived back at the cabin," he said, getting to the point. "He was digging in the cellar and left his shovel behind. I need someone out here to get fingerprints off it ASAP."

"Okay, I'll send the crime scene techs, but it's going to take a while." Paul's voice sounded grim. "There was a bad two-vehicle crash on the highway between Cody and Greybull, one dead on scene, and the other was sent to the hospital in Cody. I had to respond here rather than digging into your suspect, Ward Engler. You may have to wait for Griff to do that. Looks like I'm going to be stuck here for at least a couple of hours."

Shane suppressed a sigh. One of the reasons their SAR services were in high demand was because their local law enforcement resources were limited. "Okay, I understand. I'll close the cellar door, and we'll hang here to wait for the techs."

"Later." Paul quickly ended the call.

Shane mounted the steps, blinking as his eyes were forced to adjust to the sunlight. As he closed the cellar doors, Bryce bounded toward him. "Hand." Shane waited as Bryce dropped the ducky into his palm. "Good boy," he praised. The dog wagged his tail, acknowledging a job well done. "Come, Bryce." He turned and walked up to the house. He still needed to call his siblings, too, and hoped they could find a route to the cabin that wouldn't be blocked by the two-car crash scene.

It bothered him that he and Libby may be hanging out here at the cabin without any outside support. He stepped through the patio doors to discover that Libby had already grabbed his new computer from the SUV and had set up a temporary office at the kitchen table.

She glanced at him as he crossed over. "What took you so long?"

"The guy spent his time here digging through the back of the cellar." He crossed to the kitchen sink to pour water into a bowl for Bryce. The dog lapped at the water, then stretched out on the floor. "The good news is that he left a shovel behind. The bad news was when I called Paul, he was at the scene of a serious crash on the highway. One dead, the other seriously wounded. He won't be able to help us for a while, but he promised to send the crime scene techs to see if they can lift prints from the shovel."

Her expression turned sad. "That's awful about the crash, but surely the state police can handle it?"

He shrugged and reached for his phone. "I can only assume they're tied up with tourist stuff too." He scrolled to his sister Alexis's number and pressed the call button. She answered in two rings. "Hey, Alexis, any chance you and Joel can bring your K9s out to the cabin this afternoon? You'll have to avoid the highway, though, as it's been temporarily shut down because of a serious crash."

"Sure, we'll leave now," Alexis agreed. "Are you still thinking you need Denali to search for human remains?"

"No, but bring Denali along just in case." He agreed with Libby's thought about how the bad guys were probably keeping Marvin alive long enough to find the money. "Also, you and Joel need to pack your side arms."

"Okay, we can do that." Alexis paused, then added, "Have you reached out to Doug?"

"No, but Griff Flannery is on his way from Cheyenne." He quickly filled her in on the discovery that Libby's grandfather had stolen money from an armored truck almost fifty years ago and the recent discovery of digging being done in the cellar.

"Wow, that's crazy," Alexis said, when he'd finished. "You really should clue Doug in on what's going on. I realize this doesn't impact his job with the DEA, but he'll want to be involved if possible. Maya and Chase are still in Jackson but should be heading back soon. They found the missing hikers, and everyone is doing fine."

"Good to hear Chase and Maya had a good outcome on their search. I'll contact Doug." He glanced at his watch. It was already one o'clock in the afternoon. By the time his siblings arrived, it would be closer to two. He felt as if they were running out of time, but there wasn't anything he could do to speed things up. "Drive safe and we'll see you soon, Alexis."

"Yep. Soon," she agreed, and ended the call.

Shane sent Doug a brief text instead of calling. In truth, he didn't want to get into the whole story again. When Doug responded a moment later, he said he was tied up with a case but would call later. Shane sent the okay sign and turned back toward Libby. She was using her phone as a hot spot to access the internet. "Find anything yet?"

"I think so. This is the article about Harry being released from prison." She frowned. "There's a grainy photo here of his mug shot. Come see what you think. I can't find a good resemblance to Engler."

Shane crossed over to peer at the screen. Harry Stern had a thin, angular face with close-cropped dark hair. Picturing the round facial features of Ward Engler along with the older man's thick hair, he was inclined to agree.

"You're right. I hate to say it, but I don't think they're the same person." He frowned, wondering why on earth Engler had acted so strangely. It didn't make sense that he'd bolt from the café without a good reason. When they'd spoken at the overpass, the guy hadn't acted as if he were afraid of dogs. Then again, Engler had demanded they stay back, or he'd shoot.

"So now what?" Libby sounded dejected. "I was so sure they were one and the same man."

"Let's focus on Engler himself rather than Harry Stern," he suggested. "For one thing, we know Engler is here in the area. Harry Stern could be here, too, or he could be on the other side of the country. The fact is Engler acted suspicious. Maybe the two guys know each other, and Harry asked Engler for help. Stern may have hired Engler's kids or other relatives to help him find the money."

"Kidnappers for hire?" She grimaced. "I guess that's possible."

He was about to say anything was for hire when he heard a high-pitched engine. The minibike? Had the guy who'd been digging in the cellar decided to come back to finish the job? Maybe he'd assumed they'd taken off.

"Take the laptop into the bathroom and lock the door." He pulled his weapon and turned to find Bryce was already on his feet, his ears pricked toward the sound.

"Wait, what about you?" She grabbed his arm. "Come with me."

"I can't. Call 911 so we have backup. Bryce and I will handle this." He spoke with confidence, even though his gut was clenched with fear.

"Be safe." Libby pocketed her phone, picked up the computer and headed down the hall to the bathroom.

"Come, Bryce." He kept his voice low, listening as the high-pitched engine grew louder. There was no question in his mind that this guy was coming back.

Did he have reinforcements with him? Shane strained to listen, trying to determine whether there was more than one rider heading to the cabin.

Keeping Bryce close to his side, Shane moved through the living room to the edge of the patio doors. He took a deep breath, then peered around to the woods beyond the backyard clearing. He couldn't see anything moving, but the engine indicated the guy was close.

Bryce's ears flickered from side to side. Then he began to growl low in his throat.

The seconds ticked by slowly. Shane continued to scan the woods and thought it was strange that he didn't see any movement.

Just as he was wondering if the guy was sitting out there, waiting for someone else to arrive, he caught a glimpse of sunlight reflecting off glass.

A rifle scope? Reacting on instinct, he ducked as the crack of gunfire rang out. The patio doors shattered beneath the force of the bullet.

What in the world? Shane huddled on the floor, his arm around Bryce as another shot rang out. This time, the round penetrated the wood siding to the right of the now-shattered patio doors.

In that moment, Shane understood this guy wanted them to flee. To get as far away from the cabin as possible.

A third round punctured the wall about two feet over his head. Shane knew this guy was sitting somewhere well out of their reach, using a rifle to keep them pinned down and so that Shane couldn't send Bryce out after him.

"Heel, Bryce," he said in a low voice. In a low crouch, he moved quickly across the room and into the kitchen, taking shelter behind the cabinets. He tried to think of a way out of this mess. They had two options, stay and wait for the sheriff's department to get there or to get as far away from the cabin as possible.

"Shane?" Libby called from the bathroom. "Who's shooting at us? Are you and Bryce okay? What's going on?"

Libby's choked voice made the decision for him. If the bad guys wanted them gone, then he didn't see much of an alternative. "We're fine, but this guy isn't going to stop anytime soon. We need to make a run for it. He's hiding in the woods to the back of the house so we're going out front to the SUV."

There was a long pause before Libby responded. "Okay. I'm coming."

"Bryce, heel." Once Bryce came to his side, he dug the key fob from his pocket and double-clicked the button to start the engine. Then he quickly pushed another button to open the back hatch. The silence from the gunman was unnerving. He hoped the guy wasn't making his way closer. "Libby, we need to go!"

"I'm here." She peeked around the corner, the laptop clutched to her chest. Another round struck the back wall of the cabin, and she instinctively ducked.

There wasn't a moment to lose. He darted toward the front door and wrenched it open. Bryce stayed close, and Libby was quick to follow.

"Get inside, hurry!" He waved toward the SUV. "You, too, Bryce. Get up!"

On command, Bryce ran forward and leaped into the back crate area. Shane punched the button to close the hatch, determined to keep his dog safe. He made sure Libby was in the passenger seat before making his way to the other side and sliding in behind the wheel.

"Stay down," he advised Libby as he gunned the engine. Expecting more rounds to strike the SUV, and silently thanking his brother Chase for adding bulletproof glass to their vehicles, he sped down the driveway toward the highway as fast as possible.

13

———

Heart lodged in her throat, Libby bent over the laptop she had brought along, braced for the SUV to be riddled with bullets. Shane took a sharp turn, then hit the gas. She realized he was heading away from Greybull and Cody, toward the mountains. When the gunfire finally stopped, she lifted her head.

"Stay down," Shane barked.

Suppressing a sigh, she turned to look up at him. "I don't hear anything. It sounds like the shooting has stopped."

"For now, but who knows if there're other shooters out there?" Shane's expression could have been carved from stone. "Just stay down a while longer, okay? I knew staying at the cabin was a bad idea."

She winced. "My fault."

"Don't worry about it." Shane sounded less upset now that they were relatively safe. If there was such a thing as being safe, which she was beginning to doubt. Especially since they were no closer to finding her grandfather.

"I don't understand. Why did he start shooting?"

It took Shane a moment to respond. "I think he wanted

us gone so he could keep digging in the cellar for the treasure."

That had her sitting up. "Well then, we need to call Paul and have him head out there to arrest him."

Shane grimaced, but the call he made wasn't to Paul. The name that popped up on the dashboard screen was Alexis Sullivan. "Don't go to Marvin Tolliver's cabin," he said in a curt tone. "Some guy with a rifle has taken several shots at the place, forcing us out of there. We're back on the road."

"What in the world?" Alexis sounded shocked. "On the road heading where?"

"Don't know yet," Shane admitted. "Turn around and head for the ranch. I don't want you or Joel anywhere near the gunman. If you ask me, they're getting desperate. As if they know they're running out of time."

Libby couldn't help but agree with that sentiment. They'd had her grandfather for more than twenty-four hours. They probably hadn't anticipated it would be this difficult to get the money.

If there was any money. Libby still wasn't sure that her grandfather had kept it or if he'd used it over the course of the past forty-eight years.

"We're not going back to the ranch," Alexis said firmly. "We're coming to back you up. Tell me where you are right now."

Shane sighed. "We're heading east on Highway 14. But I don't know what our final destination is. You could be driving aimlessly for hours."

"Doesn't matter, we're heading your way," Alexis insisted. "Keep us in the loop."

"Okay, I will." Shane sounded resigned. "But whatever you do, stay away from Marvin's cabin."

"Got it. Call us back when you have a plan."

"Yeah, as soon as I think of one," Shane muttered sourly, before ending the call.

"I had an idea shortly before the gunfire erupted." Libby opened the laptop. "Hang on, I need to use my phone as a hot spot again."

He frowned as she pulled out the phone. "Okay, but what's your idea?"

"Let's see if it even works." She was hesitant to say too much because what she was about to do would get her fired. If she were caught.

Then again, her grandfather was running out of time. Without Paul or any other law enforcement helping them, she didn't have much of a choice. As Shane had mentioned, the gunmen were getting desperate. They were going to keep searching for the money until they found it.

And once they did? Her grandfather would be taken out of the picture for good.

Drawing a deep breath, she brought up the hospital billing system. She had to go through a few extra steps as the system didn't recognize her using this particular device. But it didn't take too long, and soon she was logged into the hospital billing system. From there, she quickly entered Ward Engler's name to see if he was in the system. If he wasn't, there would be nothing more she could do.

He was! Her heart thudded against her ribs as his name and address popped up on the screen. "I have Engler's address."

"You do? How?" Shane looked shocked.

"I logged into the hospital's billing system. He was treated at the hospital in Cody last year." She shrugged, then added, "I've broken all kinds of rules accessing the hospital database for personal reasons, but that doesn't matter. For now, I think we need to head over there. If nothing else, to cross him off the list of suspects once and for all."

"What's the address?" Shane asked.

She rattled it off. Using the built-in map application in his SUV computer, he found the address. He tapped the screen. "Here's the location. And surprisingly, it's not far from where we are right now."

"Which means it's not that far from Grandpa's cabin. I think we're onto something." She held Shane's gaze for a long moment. "Engler has a trailer that could have housed the four-wheelers. Then he acted guilty when you saw him in Greybull. I don't know yet how he fits into this, I don't think he looks like the bank robbery accomplice Harry Stern who is out of jail, but I'm convinced he's involved." She frowned, then added, "What's odd is that Ward Engler is a local resident. And that he doesn't live that far from Grandpa. I wouldn't have expected that."

"I agree, that's odd. But who knows how these things happen?" Shane hit a button so that the route to Engler's place was highlighted on the screen. After a few minutes, he made another call to Alexis. "Hey, we have a new plan. We're headed to the home of a guy by the name of Ward Engler."

"Who's he?" Alexis asked.

"An older guy who came to our attention yesterday when we noticed him hauling a trailer that we believe housed a couple of four-wheelers. Bryce didn't alert on Marvin's scent, so we didn't think too much of it. But I took a picture of his truck license plate and reported him to the local police. That's how we learned his name was Ward Engler. When I saw him in the town of Greybull, I thought I'd try again with Bryce, only the guy took off out the back door, leaving half his lunch behind."

"How did you get his address?" Alexis asked.

"That doesn't matter," Shane said. "But take the information down so you have it, too, okay?"

"Give it to me," Alexis agreed.

He gave her the address. "I know you're still at least an hour or so away, but we're going to find a place to park and head in on foot. Keep in mind, Bryce didn't alert initially, so I don't think Marvin Tolliver was ever in his car. This could turn out to be nothing, but we won't know until we check it out."

"Maybe you should wait for police backup," Alexis said, her voice tinged with worry. "What if this guy is armed and tries to take you and Libby out of the picture?"

"I'm armed, too, so I'm not that worried about one old guy. Besides, the police are tied up at the deadly crash scene, remember?" Shane's expression turned impatient. "We don't even know if this guy is involved. Maybe he's scared of dogs. Or maybe he took money to move the four-wheelers and that's the extent of things. If we don't find anything at his place, we'll look for a place to meet up with you and Joel."

"Okay." Alexis let out a heavy sigh. "I don't like it but will wait to hear from you."

"Thanks. One of us will be in touch." He ended the call.

"One of us?" Libby echoed with a frown. "You're not leaving me behind."

He drove in silence for a long moment. The gap between their current location and their destination, Engler's home, shrank with every mile. "I don't know what to tell you, other than I don't think we can just walk up to the front door to ask if your grandfather is there."

"Of course not." She tried not to roll her eyes. "You said you'd find a place to park so that we can go in on foot."

"Yeah. Speaking of which, zoom in on that map. See

what's around the property if you can." He gestured to the computer screen.

"Give me a minute to pull it up on the computer." She was more comfortable working off the laptop. Her car didn't have a fancy built-in computer screen like this. After a minute of examining the area, she grimaced. "Looks to me like the house is surrounded by woods on three sides, the only exception being the front, which as you pointed out isn't an option." She looked at the highway, the location of the Engler driveway, and then back at the map. "Okay, so we get off Highway 14 and take Eagle's Way Road, which leads to the property. You'll need to drive past the house for about a half mile. Looks like there's a cleared spot off the road there that we can use as a starting point."

Shane nodded and slowed the SUV as they approached Eagle's Way Road. She found herself holding her breath as he turned left and continued north. She searched their surroundings as the moving dot on the screen indicated they were approaching their target. She caught a glimpse of a dark-green house about fifty yards off the road before Shane passed it. He kept his speed steady for the next half mile, then he stopped and pulled off the road.

"I didn't see any cars in the driveway," she said as he shifted into park.

"I didn't either, but there's a huge pole barn." He shrugged. "Needs room for that trailer, the four-wheelers, and whatever other toys he's got stashed away."

Libby didn't want to admit how unnerving it was to be so close to the place. As Shane stared out the windshield, she wondered if he was having second thoughts. "I'll go," she offered.

"No." He shot her a frustrated look. "That's not happening."

Had he decided to wait for his siblings to get there? "Please, Shane, I really need to find my grandfather. Whatever he did in the past, he doesn't deserve what the kidnappers are putting him through now."

"I never said he deserved this," Shane said with a frown. "If you want to know the truth, I'm trying to decide if I should take Bryce with me."

A wave of relief hit hard when she realized he hadn't changed his mind about moving forward with the plan. "Why wouldn't you?"

"He's trained to bark when he alerts." Shane shrugged. "I can give him the command to stay silent, but that doesn't mean he won't get excited if he picks up the scent." He drummed his fingers along the top of the steering wheel. "I don't know. It may be better if I head out alone to see if anyone is even there."

She wasn't sure she liked that idea. "I'd rather you take Bryce with you. He's so well trained, I can't imagine he'll bark if you tell him not to."

A hint of a smile quirked the corner of Shane's mouth. "Okay, I'll take him." He pushed open his driver's side door. "Let's gear up."

Gear up? She wasn't sure what he meant, but she pushed out of the car to join him. He let Bryce out, then rummaged in the space beneath the crate area. She peered over his shoulder, amazed to see there were all kinds of things stuffed in what appeared to be a relatively shallow storage area.

"Here, this is for you." He held out a vest. It was heavier than she'd expected, making her realize it was made of Kevlar.

"You think we'll need these?" It was her turn to have second thoughts.

"Better to be safe than sorry." He helped her fit the Velcro straps over her torso, tugging them snug. Then he donned his vest. Lastly, he bent to attach Bryce's K9 heavy bulletproof vest.

"I'm glad he has protection too." She bent to stroke Bryce's head.

"Yeah, although dogs have a higher chance of suffering serious internal bleeding if they're struck by a bullet even with the vest on." He frowned and knelt beside Bryce. "The good news is that you're fast, right boy? A moving target is much harder to hit."

The thought of Bryce suffering internal bleeding made her feel sick to her stomach. All this because of money? Money that she wasn't even sure still existed! Was this a terrible mistake?

She couldn't bear the thought of losing her grandfather, so she pushed the doubts aside. But as Shane went through the usual routine of offering Bryce water and then getting ready to search, she lifted her heart in prayer.

Please, Lord Jesus, keep us all safe in Your care!

"I NEED you to stay close to the SUV while we're gone," Shane told Libby.

"Oh, but—" she began to protest.

"I'm not going to argue with you about this." He tried to soften his tone. "If I'm not back in thirty minutes, I want you to drive out of here. Find my siblings and the police." He held her gaze for a long moment. "Please, Libby. If something goes wrong, I need to know you'll get help here as soon as possible."

Her face paled, but she reluctantly nodded. "Okay, I'll

wait here for thirty minutes, and if you don't come back, I'll contact your siblings and the police." She frowned. "I don't have Alexis's or Joel's number."

He took a moment to make sure she entered Alexis's and Joel's numbers into her phone. Satisfied, he turned to gaze down at his dog. He debated which search scent he should have Bryce focus upon. They knew there was more than one bad guy involved. On the off chance the one bad guy Bryce had gotten a piece of had never been to Ward Engler's home, he decided to go with Marvin's scent.

"Here, Bryce." He offered the scent bag containing Marvin's dirty socks and T-shirt to his K9. After all, their mission was to find Libby's grandfather. Alerting on the bad guy without having Marvin nearby wasn't helpful. "Search Marvin!"

Bryce sniffed the bag, then looked up at him with his dark eyes as if to say *Yes, I remember.*

"Good boy," He tucked the bag back into the SUV, then lifted his finger to his mouth in a *shh* gesture. "Search Marvin," he repeated in a hushed voice. He hadn't done as much training with Bryce on doing quiet searches as that was typically not needed, but the way Bryce gazed up at him made him think the dog understood.

Yet he also knew that Bryce would only be silent as long as he didn't sense a threat. Bryce's protective instincts were such that the dog would absolutely bark and growl in warning if he caught Bad Guy's scent. Still, he was hoping they could get to the house and back without running into anyone else.

Bryce wheeled away from him and lowered his nose to the ground. Shane shot one last look at Libby standing near the SUV, resisting the urge to draw her into his arms for a kiss. As if she'd read his mind, she crossed over and wrapped her arms around him, pulling him close.

Heartened by her embrace, he couldn't help but sigh. "Ah, Libby," he whispered, before lowering his mouth to hers. She kissed him back, and it was tempting to blurt his growing feelings for her right then and there. He wasn't sure how it had happened, but she'd broken through the walls he'd built around his heart.

More like shattered them to smithereens.

Then she drew away, offering a somber smile. "Be safe, Shane."

"I promise." He forced himself to let her go, taking a step back before he gave in to the need to kiss her again. "Remember our agreement," he added. "Thirty minutes."

"Thirty minutes," she repeated in agreement. "I'll be here waiting for you."

He nodded, knowing she would be. Turning away, he quickened his pace to follow Bryce into the foliage. Bryce lowered his nose to the ground and trotted alongside him. As the woods enveloped them, Shane did his best to step as quietly as possible.

From this point forward, he couldn't afford to make any mistakes. The last thing he wanted was to be forced into a situation where he needed to use lethal force.

Bryce moved through the woods in a side-to-side pattern that told Shane the dog had not yet caught Marvin's scent. Not surprising as they weren't even close to the property. Typically, he didn't like to guide the dog in the right direction of where he needed the animal to search, but these circumstances were far from normal.

They needed to get close to the dark-green house belonging to Ward Engler. Hopefully, Bryce would alert well before they got to the house itself.

If Marvin was there. He knew full well that they were operating on little more than a weak theory based on a man who'd abandoned his meal. This trip to the Engler home may be nothing more than a wild-goose chase.

Shane pulled out his compass, making a note of the coordinates. Then he embarked on a path that was due west of his current location. Keeping an eye on the time, he subtly herded Bryce toward the property. The dark-green siding blended so well with the trees that Shane worried he'd walk right past it without ever seeing it.

He estimated they were about a hundred yards from the place when he finally caught a glimpse of a darker green between the trees. He bent and put a hand on Bryce's head, bringing the dog to a stop.

Bryce stared up at him, clearly wanting to continue the search game. He dropped to one knee, bringing the dog in close. Then he made the *shh* motion with his hand again. Bryce wagged his tail but didn't bark.

Satisfied his K9 would listen, he rose and continued to approach the property. The woods ended about twenty yards from the side of the house. His compass had led him exactly where he'd wanted to be. At least, as far as getting close to the place without being seen.

But it didn't appear as if Bryce had locked in on Marvin's scent.

He watched for a moment. Seeing no movement, he darted through the clearing until he was pressed up against the side of the house. Bryce stayed close to his side. Shane edged toward the front of the property and peeked around the corner.

Nobody was out front. He glanced at Bryce, who sniffed the air with interest. His K9 didn't alert, but it could be they brought Marvin in from the back.

If they'd carried the man in, would Bryce alert on his scent? Maybe, maybe not. His dog was good, but scents didn't linger in the air forever. Especially those outdoors where the elements caused them to dissipate relatively quickly. Wyoming was well known for its brisk wind.

Moving back to the center of the side wall, he peered into the closest window. The bedroom appeared to be empty, but the sheets on the queen-sized bed were left in a messy tangle. There were also clothes draped over a nearby chair and a lone cowboy hat sitting on top of a dresser. There was no doubt in Shane's mind the items had been left behind by the homeowner, Ward Engler.

He eased along the side of the wall to the next widow. Peering inside, he was disappointed to realize this window offered a view of the same bedroom. It occurred to him that the house may be a split-ranch model, where the main bedroom was located on one side of the house, leaving the second and third bedrooms on the opposite side.

Unfortunately, it wouldn't be easy to get to the other side of the house. Walking as quietly as possible, he headed to the corner. There he peeked around to check the back of the house. He noticed a pair of tall glass patio doors halfway down and surmised it was a similar setup to Marvin's home, where the general living room and kitchen area were situated in the middle with a view of the outside overlooking the back patio.

Probably not a good idea to go that way. He turned and went back around to the front of the house, Bryce at his side like a silent shadow. This side of the property had a concrete step leading to the front door. There was also a large picture window. Shane crept toward the window and carefully peered inside, doing his best not to be seen. It didn't take long to notice the main living space of the house was empty.

All hope of finding Marvin inside faded as he scanned the kitchen and living room that were slightly larger than what Marvin had at his cabin.

Now what?

A hint of movement caught his eye, causing him to rear back to avoid being seen. His heart thundered against his rib cage for several seconds. Taking a steadying breath, he edged closer until he could see inside again.

A short, stout figure had entered the kitchen.

Not Ward Engler, he quickly realized. A woman, roughly Ward's age or older based on the long gray hair pinned into a bun at the nape of her neck. He frowned. Somehow, he hadn't anticipated Engler would have a wife. Not that it was unusual for folks to be married. More so that he hadn't remembered Deputy Paul Holland mentioning a wife.

Clearly, she existed, as she was doing something near the kitchen sink. Maybe washing dishes? When she stood for several seconds with her back toward him, he decided to make his move.

Bending over, he quickly crossed the front of the house to reach the other side. Bryce started to follow but then stopped to sniff near the front door. Then the dog sat and turned to stare at him intently.

An alert? Most likely, and he was proud of the way his K9 didn't bark. Shane lifted his finger to his lips again to reinforce the need to be quiet, then gave Bryce the *come* hand signal. The dog bounded to his side, tail wagging as if anticipating he'd get to play with his rubber ducky.

As much as it pained him, Shane knew this wasn't the time to offer Bryce his reward. For one thing, he didn't want the dog to attract the woman's attention. More importantly, he didn't have eyes on Marvin.

In lieu of the ducky reward, he knelt beside Bryce and

rubbed his hands over the dog's head and ears, his torso was covered by the vest, and murmured encouraging words near his ears. The dog leaned into him, his tail wagging. After a long moment, he stood. Giving the dog the signal to heel, he made his way up to the next window.

As he suspected, it was another bedroom. One that appeared to be empty and unused. The bed was neatly made, and there was no clothing strewn about or shoes kicked into the corner. Clearly not a hiding spot.

He kept going until he reached the next pair of windows. As expected, this was the third and last bedroom.

This one wasn't empty! There were some clothes on a chair, but he couldn't tell if the shirt was the red plaid one Libby deduced her grandfather had been wearing when he'd been kidnapped. Shane narrowed his gaze, trying to see better. Someone was lying on the bed, a thin blanket drawn up over one shoulder as the person's face was turned toward the wall. From this angle, he couldn't tell if the person was male or female, much less make a positive ID.

Should he tap on the window to get the person's attention? Or would the noise draw the woman into the room?

As he stood debating his next move, the figure on the bed abruptly rolled over so that they were lying on their back, staring up at the ceiling.

The older man's features were drawn into a grimace, and there was a dark bruise on the side of his temple. Just to be sure, he pulled out his phone and quickly compared the image of the man on the bed with the picture of Libby's grandfather that she'd shared with him and the police.

A match. He'd found Marvin Tolliver!

14

Waiting was agonizing. Libby tried not to stare at her watch but couldn't seem to help herself. Each minute ticked by with excruciating slowness. To the point she'd wondered if the stupid watch was broken.

Only once a five full minutes had passed was she convinced time hadn't stood still.

After Shane and Bryce had disappeared into the woods, she'd strained to listen, hoping to hear their path as much as possible. The rustling movements were somewhat reassuring.

But now the woods were eerily silent, leaving her imagination to run wild. Had Shane missed the house? Found the place empty and abandoned? Or had he been caught by the bad guys?

She paced a path along the length of the SUV. No, she couldn't believe Shane had been caught. Not with Bryce on guard. The dog would alert him to danger, so she quickly pushed that possibility aside. Most likely, Shane was taking his time, creeping up to the house in silence. He'd find what they needed.

And if he didn't? She couldn't bear to consider that alternative. They needed to find something related to her grandfather's disappearance. She didn't want to consider the fact that she'd risked being fired from her job for nothing.

Not only that, but where would they go from here? They had no idea who else could be involved? Aside of the bad guy who was back at her grandfather's cabin right now, digging away in the cellar. *Not just one of them*, she thought with a frown. *Two or more.*

Whoever these guys were, they'd fired at them specifically to drive her and Shane away so they could freely access the money.

Maybe they'd even gotten closer to unburying the stolen loot than she and Shane had realized.

Again, she shook off the depressing thoughts. She glanced at her watch again and winced. Only ten minutes left of Shane's designated time frame left to go.

The silence was unnerving. Yet she also knew she wouldn't hear Bryce alert, not after the way Shane had used the hand signal to be silent. The Sullivan K9s were extremely well trained if a dog like Bryce could learn not to bark in specific situations. That was something she'd never have believed if she hadn't seen it for herself.

She paced again as the minutes ticked past.

And when she was forced to acknowledge the designated thirty minutes had passed, Libby knew she wasn't going anywhere. Not yet.

Not without Shane, Bryce, and her grandfather.

What should she do? Shane had wanted her to find his siblings. Silently agreeing that was a good place to start, she pulled out her phone and sent a text message to Alexis. *This is Libby. How close are you to the Engler property?*

Three little dots emerged on the screen, indicating Alexis was typing a reply. Then Libby's screen lit up. *Roughly 20 minutes. What's up?*

Nothing to worry about. See you soon. Libby sent the text, then slipped her phone back into her pocket. Passing the burden of her concern over the length of time Shane had been gone onto his siblings wasn't fair. She had no reason to believe he was hurt or in harm's way.

Just the opposite. The seemingly never-ending silence in the woods made her think Shane was still making his way to the property. No doubt navigating the thickly wooded terrain was taking him longer than he'd anticipated.

Or so she told herself. Better to think that than to imagine he'd gotten into a bind.

She rolled her head from side to side, trying to ease the tension that had settled between her shoulder blades. Another minute passed, making her wince. Maybe she should have taken the SUV and headed out to meet with Alexis and Joel the way Shane had asked her to.

Her phone buzzed again. She pulled out her phone, expecting to see a reply from Alexis, but instead, the message was from Shane.

I found him.

Her grandfather! *Thank you, Lord Jesus!* Libby lifted her gaze to the heavens above, thanking God for protecting her grandfather and guiding Shane to find him. Then she quickly typed a reply. *Can he walk? Or should I come to—*

"Drop the phone."

The command came out of nowhere. Libby whirled and swept her gaze over the area. A tall man with reddish hair stepped out from the trees.

The lethal-looking gun in his hand was pointed directly at her chest.

"Drop it," he repeated in a flat tone. "And keep your hands where I can see them. Don't give me a reason to shoot."

"Why would you want to kill me?" Libby didn't dare ignore his order, so she purposefully held the phone out to her side and let it drop to the ground. Then she held both of her hands up at waist height, palms forward. "I don't care about the money. I just want my grandfather back."

"Yeah, sure." He sneered. "I'm not falling for that."

She hadn't anticipated men governed by greed wouldn't understand people who weren't cut from the same cloth. She couldn't help lashing out at him. "I'm not kidding! Take all the money. All of it!" She tried to rein in the sheer desperation that gripped her by the throat. "Bring me my grandfather, and we'll move away. Out of state. Somewhere so far from here you'll never see or hear from us again."

"Where's your boyfriend and his dog?" The abrupt change in topic caught her off guard. "Get him here now!"

Libby was frozen by indecision. She didn't want this guy to know Shane was right now at the house where her grandfather was being held. The glint of her phone screen caught her eye. She quickly gestured to it. "Okay, fine. I'll call him. Just give me the chance to use my phone."

"No, I have a better idea." The man with reddish hair stepped closer. His brown eyes were tinged with malice. "Scream. Nice and loud. That will bring him running."

No! She couldn't!

"Do it!" he snapped. Then he lowered the muzzle of the gun so that it was pointed at her feet. "Shooting your foot will do the trick, don't you agree? I hear it's incredibly painful."

Libby didn't doubt for one minute that this thug would follow through on his vile threat. But that didn't mean she was going down without a fight. She lifted her chin, meeting his gaze straight on. "Okay, you want me to scream? Here goes." She drew in a deep breath, then shouted as loudly as possible, "Shane, don't come back!"

The gunman scowled. "I'll show you . . ." he growled.

Without waiting for him to finish, she dove to the left, trying to seek shelter behind the SUV. The move was only a temporary reprieve, but she couldn't come up with anything better. She landed on the ground hard enough to make her teeth rattle. Tucking herself into a ball, she rolled closer to the SUV. It took her a moment to remember she was wearing a vest.

Not that she was eager to test out the effectiveness of the thing. Remembering what Shane had said about bullets striking a vest causing internal bleeding convinced her it would be better to avoid being shot at all.

Still, it was strange the gunman hadn't noticed. Unless he hadn't much cared. For all she knew, bullets fired at close range could still get through.

"You think that's funny?" *Crack!* She flinched and curled herself into a tighter ball as he fired the gun. "Take this." *Crack!* "And this!" *Crack!* "There, are you happy now?" *Crack!*

Her heart was pounding so fast she thought it would have burst free of her chest. Yet oddly, she didn't feel any pain.

Lifting her head just a bit, she realized what he'd done. All four tires of the SUV were flat, having been punctured by the four bullets he'd fired.

What little defiance she'd had deflated much like the air from the tires. There was no way to escape the gunman now.

Worse, Libby knew that if she and Shane died here

today, it was her fault for not leaving at the thirty-minute mark like she'd been told.

All she could do now was to pray.

Lord Jesus, protect us all!

Libby's shouting at him to stay away sent a shaft of fear spearing through him. Especially when her shout was punctuated by four sharp gunshots.

He'd already ducked away from the house. He'd waved at the window for a full minute before he'd gotten Marvin's attention. The older man's expression had brightened with hope, but the expression didn't last long as he lifted his bound hands together as a way to explain why he hadn't tried to escape.

Shane had nodded and moved back toward the trees, hoping to regroup long enough to come up with a plan to get Marvin out of the house.

Until Libby's scream had indicated the situation had changed.

Libby wasn't armed, so someone else was there firing the gun. *Not at her*, he silently pleaded. *Please, Lord, not at Libby!*

The sound of a door opening caught his attention. Realizing the woman must have come outside in response to the gunfire, he darted through the woods for a better look. He had to assume she was armed the way most women in these parts could hold their own when it came to weapons.

But she wasn't!

"Get her!" he commanded Bryce.

The dog shot forward, moving so quietly that he was on the woman before she understood what was happening. She let out a cry when Bryce jumped up, planting his front paws on her chest. The weight of the hundred-pound dog striking with the force of a freight train bowled her over.

Shane ran forward. "Good boy! Hold, Bryce. Hold!"

Bryce stayed where he was, growling low in his throat, his snout mere inches from the woman's nose. Shane knelt beside her, doing a quick pat down to ensure she didn't have a knife or a gun tucked away.

"Release, Bryce. Release."

The dog almost looked disappointed but backed off the woman as ordered. Shane held his weapon trained on her. "Get up and walk inside. Nice and slow. Or I'll sic Bryce on you again."

"You—can't barge in here," she sputtered.

"Yes, I can. That's Marvin Tolliver you have tied up in the third bedroom." Shane gave her a not-so-gentle nudge with his foot. "Get up!"

"Okay, okay." She rolled onto her hands and knees, then rose to her feet. Her bun hung at a lopsided angle from the force of her hitting the ground. Bryce stayed at his side in the heel position as he followed the woman inside.

"Sit down." He gestured to the chair. The woman gingerly sat, as if her body hurt from the tumble. "Guard, Bryce."

Bryce trotted over and then dropped into a tall sitting position directly in front of her. The woman reared back, as if fearing he'd lunge forward. Bryce simply sat there, staring up at her, clearly waiting for his next command.

"Don't move or I'll order him to attack." It was mostly an empty threat, but there wasn't time to waste. Shane darted into the bedroom where Marvin Tolliver waited. He pulled his knife and quickly slit through the twine around his wrists.

"Wh-who are you?" Marvin stammered.

"Shane Sullivan and I'm here with my K9, Bryce." He helped the older man to his feet. "There isn't time to explain everything. We need to move. Libby is in trouble."

"My fault." Distress filled Marvin's eyes. "It's all my fault!"

"We know about the robbery. Can you walk?" Shane debated leaving the old man here so that he could get to Libby. "Come on, we need to hurry."

"Yes. I can walk." He had to admire the older man's determination.

Shane picked up the twine he'd cut from Marvin's wrists and carried it to the kitchen. The woman he assumed was Engler's wife was sitting as far back in the chair as possible, shaking with fear. He'd feel guilty about scaring her, if not for the fact that she was involved in this up to her neck.

It didn't take him long to bind her wrists together. "Get back, Bryce," he commanded. "Get back."

The dog stood and backed away from the chair, although Bryce's dark eyes continued watching his quarry. If she tried anything, Bryce would be back on her in a heartbeat.

Marvin had helped himself to a drink of water as he'd worked. He had no idea how much food or water they'd provided the older man, and that concerned him.

"You okay?" Shane asked.

"I'll make it. Let's go." Marvin wiped his mouth with his sleeve.

"Come, Bryce." Shane headed back outside with Bryce and Marvin following behind. He wanted to rush toward the SUV but knew it was likely the gunman was holding Libby hostage.

Shane grimly hoped it wouldn't come down to a demand

to give one hostage up for another. Because if he was put in that position, he'd want to protect Libby at all costs.

Yet sacrificing Marvin meant Libby would never forgive him.

"This way." He tugged Marvin's arm so that they were heading into the woods but at an angle that would take them closer to the road. The best way to avoid the hostage swap was to minimize the options.

He urged Marvin toward a cluster of trees. The old man was breathing heavily, and they'd barely gone twenty yards.

Not good. Shane gently pushed the older man to the ground. "Sit for a minute."

Marvin shook his head stubbornly. "We have to find Libby."

"I know where she is." Or so he hoped. "Listen, I need you to be strong, okay?" He held Marvin's gaze. "Eagle's Way Road isn't too far from here. Head due south and you'll walk right into it."

"That's where Libby is?" Marvin's expression was hopeful. So much so that he hated to disappoint the guy.

"Not exactly." He offered a reassuring smile. "But my siblings Alexis and Joel are on their way. Just wait for them at the road, okay? I'll take Bryce to find Libby."

Realization finally dawned. "You want me out of the way."

"Yes, I do." Shane wasn't going to lie. "And just as important, I want you to be safe. So please, move at your own pace through the trees until you reach the road. Then find a spot to stay well hidden until you see the two K9 SUVs. You'll be able to see the crates in the back for their respective dogs. Run out into the road and wave them down. Understand?"

"Yes." Marvin waved a hand. "Go. Hurry!"

"Come, Bryce." Shane squelched a flash of guilt at

leaving Marvin to make his own way out of there. As he moved quickly through the woods in a parallel path toward the SUV, he was hit by a fresh wave of fear over Libby's fate.

He couldn't bring himself to think the worst. Much the way Libby had clung to hope regarding her grandfather still being alive, he did the same thing now.

With his compass as a guide, he traversed the wooded land as quickly yet silently as possible. When he heard voices, he froze and gave Bryce the hand signal to stop.

"Scream, for real this time," a deep voice said.

"There's no point." Libby sounded exhausted. "Shane must be far away from here, or he'd have come running at the sound of gunfire."

Hearing Libby's sweet voice brought a wave of relief that made his knees go weak. She was alive!

Shane drew in a slow, steady breath and tried to come up with a plan. Despite how he'd sent Marvin to the road to meet his siblings, he honestly didn't think Alexis and Joel would get there in time to be of help.

He and Bryce would have to figure this out on their own.

"You think you're so smart?" The low, harsh voice abruptly changed. "If you're out there, Shane, you have exactly sixty seconds to show yourself. If you don't, I'll plant bullets where they'll hurt her without killing her outright. Do you hear me?" The last four words were thundered so loudly Shane was pretty sure half the mountainside could have heard them.

Including Marvin? He hoped not.

He edged closer, trying to figure out where the gunman was standing.

"Fifty-nine, fifty-eight, fifty-seven . . ." The countdown had begun.

He continued moving through the trees, keeping Bryce

in the heel position at his side. If he had no choice but to show himself, he wouldn't bring his dog.

"Forty-eight, forty-seven, forty-six," the calm voice continued.

There was no point in dragging this all the way out. Shane couldn't see the bad guy through the trees, but he could see the glint of sunlight bouncing off the windshield. He figured the gunman must have been using the SUV for cover while keeping Libby glued to his side.

"Okay! I'm coming! Don't shoot!" Shane thought he heard Libby gasp. "I'm coming! There's no reason to hurt her."

"Oh, there's every reason," the male voice said. "You and your girlfriend have been thorns in our side long enough."

Shane gave Bryce the command hand signal to stay, tucked the gun in the small of his back, then quickly ran from the woods into the clearing near the SUV with his hands up so the gunman would assume he wasn't armed. His heart sank when he realized the vehicle was sitting low to the ground because all four tires were flat.

Four shots, four tires, he thought with a sigh. "I'm here. Where's Libby?"

The gunman finally pushed Libby out from behind the SUV so that Shane could see her. He raked his gaze over her, grateful he didn't see any blood. Her gaze was full of remorse, so he offered a reassuring smile. "Are you okay? He hasn't hurt you?"

"I told you to stay back." She winced when the gunman's hand tightened painfully around her upper arm.

"Shut up." The gunman pointed his weapon at Shane. "Where's the dog?"

Shane arched a brow. "Your gunfire spooked him. He took off into the woods. I doubt he'll be back anytime soon."

The gunman stared at him for a long second. "If I find out you're lying, I'll track the dog down and kill him myself."

"Hey, you're the one who fired four shots in a row." Shane jerked his thumb toward the SUV. "Overkill, don't you think?"

"Shut up!" Clearly the red-haired man was losing his patience. Shane stared at the guy, struck by an odd sense of familiarity. He didn't remember ever meeting the guy before or seeing him, as he'd never gotten a good look at the shooter's face. Still, there was something about him that niggled at the back of his mind. "Start walking."

"And go where?" Shane didn't want to turn around lest the gunman notice the gun he had tucked into the small of his back. The guy was too close to Libby for him to make a move, so he tried to stall for more time. "We don't know our way around in these woods."

"That's the point." The guy flashed him a wow-you're-so-stupid look. "Now! I'm done playing around."

"Okay, okay." Shane took several steps to the side. When the red-haired guy scowled, he stumbled on purpose, lifting both his hands in a gesture meant to calm the guy down. "Sorry. I'm just nervous."

"I shoulda got rid of you both a long time ago," red-haired guy muttered. For the first time since Shane had walked into the clearing, the guy allowed the gun in his hand to dip toward the ground.

It was the break he'd needed. Granted, the situation was far from ideal, but he didn't hesitate to give Bryce the hand signal for attack. Like a streak of lightning, his tan and brown German shepherd bolted from the woods making a beeline for the gunman. Because Bryce had moved so silently, it took a moment for the red-haired guy to register what was happening. But not for long. The guy let out a grunt and quickly brought the business end of his gun up, aiming at Bryce.

Shane grabbed his weapon, knowing he was going to be too late. But then Libby threw herself at the red-haired man, thrusting his gun hand upward just as he pulled the trigger. "No! she shouted.

"Look out!" Shane desperately needed Libby to get out of the way. He finally had his weapon in hand but couldn't take a shot. Bryce launched himself at the red-haired guy, his front paws planted squarely on his chest, but with Libby so close, the three of them ended up on the ground in a tangle of limbs, the gun, and Bryce's sharp teeth.

"Owww, get him off!" the red-haired guy screamed.

After what seemed like an eternity, but was only a few seconds, Libby rolled away, cradling her wrist in her hand. He caught a glimpse of blood but forced himself to stay focused on the gunman.

"Get him off!" the guy screamed again.

Shane rushed forward, relieved to see that Bryce had clamped his jaw around the guy's gun hand. He leaned in and quickly wrenched the gun free.

"Hold, Bryce. Hold." Now that he had the bad guy's weapon, he turned toward Libby. "Are you okay? I saw you were bleeding."

"Fine. Just a scratch." Her smile was weak. "I know he didn't mean to bite me on purpose. Bryce just happens to have really sharp teeth."

He remembered how she'd been afraid of his imposing K9 the first time they'd met. The good news was that she didn't look too upset. He wished he'd thought to bring additional rope from the house, but there hadn't been time. He backed up a few steps, then said, "Release, Bryce. Release."

The dog let go of the red-haired man's arm and backed

up. But the way Bryce stared at the red-haired guy indicated the dog viewed him as a threat. "Don't try anything or I'll have him attack again. Only this time I'll make sure he grabs your neck with his teeth."

The red-haired guy scrambled backward across the ground, as if desperate to put distance between them.

"Guard, Bryce," Shane said firmly. "Guard."

Bryce stood in front of the red-haired guy, his unblinking gaze zeroed in on the bad guy's face. The look of fear in the bad guy's features provided a grim satisfaction.

"Where's my grandfather?" Libby pinned Shane with an anxious gaze. "Is he okay?"

"I'm here, Libby." To Shane's shock, Marvin's voice came from the side of the SUV closest to the road.

"Are you hurt, Marvin?" Shane didn't dare take his gaze from the red-haired guy in case this was some sort of trick. "Why didn't you go to the road the way I asked?"

"Because it's my fault." Marvin sounded incredibly weary. "And I needed to make sure Libby and Aaron didn't hurt each other."

"Aaron?" It took a moment for him to realize Marvin knew his kidnappers by name. Which shouldn't have surprised him, considering Libby's grandfather had obviously known his accomplices back when they committed the armored truck robbery in the first place.

"Aaron and Archer are my sister's twin grandsons," Marvin said. "And they're here because they want the money."

His sister? Shane understood then that Aaron and Archer were Libby's second cousins.

15

Libby whirled around to stare at her grandfather, her injured arm forgotten. She should have considered her great-aunt might be involved. After all, that was the match she'd found on the DNA test she'd submitted to the database. And looking at Aaron's red hair, similar in color to hers, she couldn't help feeling sick about the family connection.

One she hadn't anticipated.

"Grandpa." She rushed over to wrap her arms around him in a hug, grateful he was alive and relatively unhurt. "I'm sorry it took us so long to find you."

"I'm fine." He returned her embrace, although with less strength than usual. "Better now that I know you're not hurt either."

"Grandpa, why didn't you tell me?" She leaned back to search his gaze. "All these years . . ."

"It's a long story, Libby." Her grandfather looked fragile and weary.

"Let's have you sit down." She led her grandpa toward the useless SUV. She opened the passenger-side door and urged him to sit. "Are you sure you're okay?" He looked so pale she wondered when he had last had anything to eat or drink.

"I'll survive." Grandpa turned to look at Shane. "How much longer until your siblings get here?"

Shane shrugged and glanced at her. She nodded, silently letting him know she'd been in touch.

"I texted with Alexis about fifteen minutes ago." Libby double-checked her phone. "At that point in time, they were twenty minutes out. I'm sure they'll be here very soon."

"Good to know." Shane kept his pistol leveled at Aaron. "I left a woman who I assume is Ward Engler's wife tied up back at the Engler home. I don't know how the Englers are involved, but it's clear they are. Is Archer the one digging in the cellar?"

"Probably," Grandpa agreed. "I told Archer and Aaron that's where I hid the money."

She frowned. "You still have the cash? You never used it for yourself?"

Her grandfather winced. "I did use some in the beginning. I had to escape, get a new identity, and relocate here to Wyoming from Colorado." He shrugged and let out a heavy sigh. "As I said, it's a long story."

She wanted to point out that they had plenty of time to hear what had transpired all those years ago, but she realized her grandfather might not want to say too much in front of Aaron.

Or maybe he didn't want to incriminate himself more than he already had.

Libby hated knowing there was a strong possibility her grandfather would end up in jail. Forty-eight years was a long time, but one man and a cop had been killed during the robbery. And there was no statute of limitations on murder.

Her phone buzzed with an incoming call. Seeing Alexis's name on the screen, she quickly answered. "Shane found Grandpa, and we also have one of the bad guys here. There's at least one more out there, though. Maybe more."

"I'm glad Shane found your grandfather. We're coming up on your coordinates right now," Alexis said. "Oh, and you should know FBI agent Griff Flannery is on his way to your grandfather's place right now."

"You better warn him that a man named Archer is likely digging in the cellar there," Libby said somberly. "He should be considered armed and dangerous."

"I will, thanks." Alexis ended the call.

Libby lowered the phone, her gaze narrowing on Aaron. His arm was bloody from where Bryce had latched onto him, but as her gaze traveled down his jean-clad legs, she didn't see any evidence of ripped denim indicating he was the one Bryce had gotten a piece of earlier that morning.

She turned toward Shane. "I think Archer must be the one with the dog bite on his leg."

"I agree." Shane glared at Aaron. "You and your brother are going away for a long time."

Aaron looked away without saying anything in response. Hearing a car engine, Libby turned in time to see two SUVs rolling over the terrain toward them.

Leaving her grandfather's side, she hurried over to meet them. Alexis slid out from behind the wheel, glancing at Shane first as if to make sure her brother was really okay, then to where her grandfather was sitting in the passenger seat.

"Alexis, can you tie this guy up for me?" Shane asked. "He'll probably need to be seen at the hospital for his dog bite. Libby, too, as she deflected his gun arm only to get tangled with Bryce's teeth."

"Sure thing." Alexis rummaged around in the back of her SUV reassuring her K9, Denali, that they'd be fine. Seconds later, she used plastic zip ties to bind Aaron's wrists together.

"Thanks." Shane finally lowered the gun. "Here, Bryce."

The large German shepherd wheeled away from Aaron to trot to Shane's side. Shane knelt beside his dog, ruffling and stroking his fur. "You're a good boy, aren't you? Good boy."

Libby wanted to believe the nightmare was over, but there were too many questions without answers. When the sharp crack of gunfire rang out in the distance, she, Shane, Alexis, and Joel all exchanged horrified looks.

"Griff! That sounds as if it could have come from Marvin's cabin," Alexis cried out in horror. "We need to head back there."

"We're coming with you," Shane said, hurrying over to join her. "Our SUV isn't going anywhere."

"I'll take this guy with me," Joel said, jerking his thumb at Aaron, "and we'll meet you at the cabin."

It didn't take long for Alexis to jump behind the wheel of her SUV. Libby helped her grandfather into the passenger seat of Alexis's car. She, Shane, and Bryce crowded into the back seat. Denali pressed her nose against the crate to sniff at Bryce. The two dogs touched noses, then Bryce settled down beside Shane.

Nobody said anything as Alexis backed away from the scene, the SUV rocking and rolling over the uneven terrain. Then she turned around and headed back toward Libby's grandfather's cabin. Alexis's expression was stricken with fear and dread.

Libby could relate to the woman's concern. As Alexis kept her food on the gas pedal, the SUV covering the miles, Libby found herself praying for Griff and whoever else he'd taken with him to her grandfather's cabin.

She couldn't bear the idea of her cousin killing a federal agent. Especially over stolen money!

When Libby's grandfather's cabin came into view, she saw three different police cars in the driveway, two sheriff's deputy squads and one black SUV with red and blue lights flashing along the top. Libby assumed that one belonged to the federal agent. Alexis barreled down the driveway, bringing the Sullivan SUV to a jarring stop. Then without waiting for anyone to respond, she bolted out of the car and ran toward the house.

"Alexis!" Shane sounded irritated as he pushed out of the car to follow. Bryce bounded out to join the fray. "Alexis, stay back!"

"Griff!" Alexis shouted. Libby followed Shane and Bryce around the corner of the house toward the backyard where the cellar was located.

"I'm fine," a male voice called. "But we need an ambulance. Paul Holland took a slug to the vest."

Paul? Libby slowed to a stop as she took in the scene. A man with close-cropped reddish hair was sprawled on the ground, not moving. Deputy Paul Holland was sitting on the ground, holding a hand to his chest. Griff had his weapon trained on another man whom she quickly recognized as Ward Engler. Another deputy was in the process of slapping cuffs around Engler's wrists while reading him his rights.

"I'm glad you're okay," Alexis said, slowing to a stop. After giving Griff one last look, Alexis abruptly turned to check on Paul, crossing over to kneel beside him. "I'm well versed in first aid. Did the slug penetrate the vest?"

"I don't think so," Paul groused. "But it feels like I was kicked in the chest by a buffalo."

"I've heard it's painful," Alexis murmured as she removed the Velcro straps of the vest for a closer look. "You're going to have a whopping bruise here. But the good news is that your vest saved your life."

"Yeah, I know." Paul glanced from Alexis over to Libby. "Your grandfather?"

"He's safe." She turned to see her grandfather trudging toward them, his shoulders slumped as if he carried the weight of the world on them.

And maybe he did. A decision that had been made forty-eight years ago had caused this mess. A police officer had almost been shot and killed here today. Just like the officer who'd lost his life all those years ago.

"Grandpa?" She crossed over to put her arm around his waist. "Let's get you inside. We can find something for you to eat."

"Not yet, Libby." He awkwardly patted her arm, then pushed forward until he stood beside Griff Flannery. "I believe you've been looking for me."

Griff nodded, the sun glinting off his short blond hair. "Is your real name Maxwell Tucker?"

"Yes." Her grandfather gestured toward Ward Engler. "I believe that man is related to the man who married my sister, Louise. She must have married him after her husband, Greg Olson, was killed during the robbery. Louise and Greg had one son who in turn had the twins, Aaron and Archer." The older man winced again. "Aaron told me how my sister talked nonstop about the money she should have had. I guess that's when the twins came up with this plan to kidnap me so they could find the cash."

"Ward Engler is not an alias?" Griff asked in surprise.

"I don't think so. I think Ward and his wife, Tabitha, were asked to provide their home and the four-wheelers for money. Sounded as if Tabitha went off to visit her grandkids until everything was finished." Her grandfather frowned. "I didn't know my sister remarried, much less that she had twin grandsons that were only a few years older than Libby." He slowly shook his head. "If we had gotten away clean, we'd have split the money equally between us. But the robbery went bad, especially after my brother-in-law exchanged gunfire with the first officer who arrived on scene back then. I was the only one who got away."

"And you still have the money?" Griff asked. "Archer there was determined to dig all the way to China to find it."

"Yes, I still have most of the money." Her grandfather glanced at her warily. "I can show you where it is."

"You didn't hide it in the cellar at all, did you?" Shane asked.

"Nope." Her grandfather turned and led the way inside the cabin. She was surprised when he went down the hall to his bedroom. She, Shane, Bryce, and Griff crowded around as he pushed at the end of the bed. Her grandfather gestured to the wooden floor. At first, she didn't understand what he was pointing out.

Then she noticed the very faint outline of a square etched in the flooring. A trap door!

"One of you should probably grab a knife to pry along the edges," Grandpa said wearily. "I haven't been down there in well over thirty-five years."

"I'll get it." Griff ducked back down the hall toward the kitchen. Libby exchanged a long look with Shane until Griff returned. He knelt on the floor, used the knife, and soon had the trap door open.

Libby leaned forward to see an old canvas bag tucked into the opening. Griff reached down and opened it.

Stacks of hundred-dollar bills were bound together with plastic, looking as crisp and new as the day her grandfather had stolen them.

SHANE COULD HARDLY BELIEVE the money had been lying beneath Marvin's bed all this time. Bryce sniffed the cash with interest. Shane wanted to congratulate the wily older man for using the cellar as a ruse.

But the look of horror on Libby's face stopped him. She abruptly turned and bolted from the bedroom.

"I'm willing to accept responsibility for my actions." Marvin's expression was grim, but Shane thought he could also see a sense of relief in the man's dark eyes. As if Libby's grandfather was glad the truth was finally out in the open. "The robbery wasn't my idea. Greg was the one who put everything together. Greg's greed was one of the reasons I never reached out to my sister all this time. I knew she was the one pushing Greg to get more money. To give her the life she felt she deserved."

Shane could easily see how that may have played out. "But you didn't stop the robbery from taking place," he felt compelled to point out.

"No, and that was my biggest sin," Marvin admitted. "I went along with the plan. But after Greg was killed along with that police officer, and Harry went to prison, I decided to go straight."

"Except for the part where you never turned over the stolen money," Griff drawled.

"That's true." Marvin waved at the opening. "Our total

haul was about two million. I probably spent about sixty grand. The rest is there. As I mentioned before, I only took enough to make a fresh start."

Libby suddenly returned, her dark eyes flashing. "Don't say anything more, Grandpa. Not until we get you a lawyer."

"Ah, Libby. That's not necessary." Marvin managed a sad smile. "As the young federal agent has pointed out, I should have come forward a long time ago."

"Actually, your granddaughter is right," Griff said. "You have the right to remain silent. And to an attorney."

"I'm waiving my rights." Now a hint of steel lined the older man's tone. "I just showed you the proof of the robbery."

"Grandpa, please," Libby begged.

"No, Libby." Marvin shook his head. "I appreciate your support, but this is my mess." He frowned, then added, "I always suspected the past would come back to haunt me. Those first few years after Harry Stern was released, I looked over my shoulder all the time. But Louise sending her grandkids to take me out?" He grimaced. "That was a shock."

"I never should have done that DNA test." Libby's brown eyes filled with tears. "If I had just let it go . . ."

"It's not your fault, Libby. I believe this happened for a reason." Marvin reached over to pat her arm. "I feel better knowing Louise and her grandkids will be held accountable for their crimes too."

Libby wiped at her eyes and managed to nod. "I'll be there for you, Grandpa. Every step of the way."

"No need," Marvin said with a frown. "This is my problem. Not yours."

Shane put his arm around Libby's shoulders. "We'll be here for you, Marvin."

Libby gratefully leaned against him. "Thank you."

"Anytime." He understood there was no way she was going to leave her grandfather hanging in the wind. Yet he admired the older man for owning up to his mistakes.

"Okay, let's get you, the cash, and the two men in custody out of here," Griff said.

"Oh, and I left a woman who could be Louise tied up at the Engler home," Shane added.

"Yeah, that's my sister, Louise," Marvin said. "She made it clear she couldn't wait to get rid of me once her grandkids had the money they deserved. I think Ward Engler was getting irritated with his role in this, though. He wanted them to find the cash, pay him, and get out of there."

Shane felt Libby shiver beside him. He hugged her again, wordlessly reassuring her that everything would be okay.

"I'm afraid you'll have to leave the house too," Griff said as he slung the bag of cash over his shoulder and took Marvin's arm. "This will need to be processed as a crime scene."

"Come on, Libby, I'll drive you home," Shane offered. He gave the dog the hand signal for come. Then remembering his SUV with four flat tires, he added, "Wait, I'll have Alexis drive us back to your place in Cody."

"Okay." Libby looked completely dejected. He tried to think of a way to cheer her up but couldn't come up with anything helpful.

Her grandfather was alive, which was great. But if the older man ended up spending what was left of his life in jail, then he had a feeling Libby wouldn't be able to bounce back to her usual cheerful self.

Their roles had been switched big time.

"Sure, I'll drive you, Bryce and Libby back to Cody,"

Alexis agreed a few minutes later. "Joel has asked Justin to buy four new tires and to head out here so they can fix your vehicle."

"That would be great, thanks." The SUV wasn't his top concern, not with the way Libby looked if she'd lost her best friend. His heart ached for her.

The trip back to Cody was quiet. Libby closed her eyes as if she'd fallen asleep, but Shane didn't think she was resting the way Bryce was.

More likely, she was replaying the events over the past few days wondering if there was something they could have done differently to prevent the outcome.

Yet he personally agreed with Marvin's assessment that things had worked out this way for a reason. Libby had clung to her faith over the past thirty-six hours. He didn't want to see her give up now.

When Alexis finally pulled into Libby's driveway, the hour was going on five in the evening. Shane's stomach rumbled with hunger, and he borrowed some dog food and dishes from Alexis so he could feed Bryce.

Once his dog was cared for, he decided to order a pizza delivery rather than rummaging through Libby's fridge.

"You don't have to stay," Libby said with a sigh. Bryce stretched out on the floor, resting his head between his paws. "There's nothing you can do, Shane."

"I'm not leaving." He held up his phone to show her the pizza he planned to order. "What do you like on your pizza?"

"I'm not hungry."

"Libby, starving yourself isn't going to help your grandfather." He scowled at her. "What do you like?"

"Pepperoni and mushrooms." She rubbed a hand over

her stomach. "I feel sick, but that could be because I'm hungry."

He placed the order, then crossed over to sit beside her on the sofa. "Let me take a look at your arm."

She showed him the long scratch marks made by Bryce's teeth. "I'll clean this up for you, okay?"

"I can do it." She looked stubborn, but he was already striding into the kitchen for water, soap, and towels.

The scratches weren't as deep as he'd anticipated, but she still might have needed antibiotics. Without a car, they would have to walk to the hospital. Or wait until morning.

"Thanks." Libby tugged her arm free. "I'll be fine."

Her listless tone bothered him. He set the items aside and turned on the sofa to face her. "Listen to me, I need you to look on the bright side."

"On the bright side of my grandfather being in jail?" Libby asked.

"Yes. He's not dead, and if you ask me, I believe he's relieved to have the truth out there." Shane took both of her hands in his. "Come on, Libby, your grandfather needs that sunshine personality of yours to help him through this."

"I know." She tipped her head back to look up at the ceiling for a minute. "I know you're right. And that nobody should get away with a crime like this without some sort of punishment. It's just..."

"You love him. But we will also be there for him, Libby. Both of us." He wanted to tell her how he'd fallen in love with her, but obviously, the timing wasn't great. He glanced around her small home. "I'll sleep here on the sofa until we hear what's going to happen."

"You would do that for me?" Libby asked, her dark-brown eyes clinging to his. "Even though I'm the granddaughter of a bank robber?"

"Armored truck robber," he corrected with a wry grin. "And hey, I give your grandfather a lot of credit for not spending the money and for turning his life around."

A reluctant smile tugged at the corner of her mouth. "I can't believe Grandpa slept every single night with almost two million dollars under his bed."

"Exactly. Can you imagine the willpower he must have had to accomplish that?" He chuckled, shaking his head. "I admire him. He never took the easy way out."

"Grandpa always told me money can't buy happiness," Libby said, her expression thoughtful. "And I always figured that was an easy thing to say if you didn't have any money to begin with. But now I realize he was right. Because we were happy. We didn't need a million dollars. We had all the love and caring we needed with each other."

"Your grandfather is a smart man." He thought about the multimillion-dollar estate he and his siblings had inherited when their parents had died. The money had been more of a pain in the behind than anything, and he had been grateful for how Maya and Chase had restructured the estate to support the ranch and their mission of offering search and rescue missions.

And in that moment, he knew if he had to choose between his inheritance and Libby, he'd walk away from the Sullivan ranch without a backward glance.

Libby was more important than anything.

"I love you." The words popped out of his mouth before he could call them back. When her eyes widened in shock, he quickly added, "Sorry, I know this is too soon for you, and rotten timing overall, but I wanted you to know. You don't have to say anything now," he quickly added. "I should have kept my big mouth shut. We'll have time after we know about what will happen to your grandfather to discuss the future."

"Oh, Shane." Libby's eyes filled with tears, and for a horrible moment, he thought she was going to tell him she didn't feel the same way. "That's the nicest thing you could have said to me."

"Which part?" He was confused over why she was crying. "That I should have kept my big mouth shut?"

That made her smile. "No, silly, the part where you told me we can wait until we know what's happening with my grandfather before we discuss the future."

"Oh, well of course." Relief hit hard. "I understand how much you love him."

"I love you, too, Shane." She shifted closer to him on the sofa. "You put your life on the line for me and my grandfather."

"You put your life on the line for Bryce," he reminded her. At his name, his shepherd lifted his head to look at them, then lowered it again as if he couldn't be bothered to move. "I couldn't believe you risked getting bitten to save him."

"I'm not afraid of Bryce." This time, Bryce rose at the sound of his name and padded toward them. Libby leaned forward to pet him. "I have to say, Bryce is an amazing dog. I can understand why you use him and the other dogs to help find people."

"We like helping others, like you, Libby. And your grandfather." Bryce nudged him, looking for more attention. "Okay, lie down, big guy." When the dog huffed and stretched out at their feet, he drew Libby in for a kiss.

"I love you, Libby," he whispered, cradling her close.

"I love you too." She kissed him again, only to jump back

in shock when Bryce leaped to his feet to bark like a maniac. "What's going on?"

"I think our pizza is here." Shane rose and pushed past Bryce, digging cash from his pocket. "You'll get used to Bryce sending up an alarm like this."

"I'm not sure about that," Libby groused, holding a hand over her chest. "He about gave me a heart attack."

"Stop, Bryce," he commanded, before opening the door. He paid the delivery man and carried the pizza inside. "Come on, Libby. Let's pray."

She crossed over to join him at the table. He took her hand and bowed his head. "Dear Lord Jesus, we thank You for this food we are about to eat. We thank You for keeping us safe in Your care today. We know You have already forgiven our sins and Marvin's too. We only ask that the judge shows Marvin mercy over his past mistakes. Amen."

"Amen," Libby echoed. "That was a beautiful prayer."

"We're going to help your grandfather through this, you'll see." He leaned in to steal another quick kiss.

"I believe you're right about that." Libby smiled, some of her cheerful attitude finally shining through. "Because with love, anything is possible."

EPILOGUE

hree weeks later . . .

Libby stood beside her grandfather in the church vestibule as the last of the wedding guests were seated. She wasn't nervous despite knowing Shane waited for her at the altar. Getting married so quickly had caused a stir in the community for just about everyone except the Sullivan family.

Oddly, Shane's eight siblings had taken their whirlwind engagement in stride. She'd expected to be talked to about waiting for a while, but that hadn't happened. Just the opposite. Everyone had been thrilled to be attending another Sullivan wedding.

Libby had known the minute Griff had announced that her grandfather would be released from custody on his own recognizance that she would take advantage of every moment they had together.

And that included having her grandfather walk her down the aisle at her wedding. Rather than waiting a few months as planned, she'd asked Shane if they could move the wedding date up. He'd been more than happy to accommodate her request.

Griff had mentioned that the statute of limitations had run on the robbery itself but that the Colorado FBI wanted to reexamine the circumstances around the deaths of both the officer who'd died in the line of duty that day and Greg Olson. Grandpa had insisted Greg had been the one to exchange gunfire with the police officer who'd died that day. She believed him, but the feds were determined to relook at the sequence of events for themselves.

Based on that, Libby had decided there wasn't a moment to waste. Her grandfather had come from jail in remarkably good spirits despite everything. And she understood that she inherited her constant cheerfulness from him.

"Are you sure about this?" Grandpa asked as they waited for the music to switch to the wedding march. "There's no reason to rush into marriage on my account."

"I'm sure," Libby said without doubt. "I love Shane, Grandpa. He's a wonderful man who has been supportive of us since the day I called and asked for his help. You're free now, and I want you to be able to spend as much time with us as possible."

"Aw, Libby." Grandpa bent and kissed her cheek. "I'm so glad you found a man like Shane Sullivan. I feel very blessed to have you in my life."

"I've been blessed to have you, too, Grandpa. I love you very much." She had to blink away the tears. This was a happy day. A day for new beginnings. To expand her family to include her grandfather and the Sullivan siblings.

And their spouses and kids, she added wryly. Talk about a noisy bunch. Yet despite their joking and teasing, she had been humbled at how the Sullivans had welcomed her grandfather into the fold without passing judgment on his past actions.

The music swelled. Libby subtly wiped at her eyes and tucked her hand in the crook of her grandfather's elbow. "That's our cue, Grandpa. Let's do this."

He nodded, covering her hand with his as he escorted her down the aisle. Shane stood in a dark suit, his smile widening when he saw her coming toward him. The warmth of his gaze was more than she could have asked for. Yet he only waited until she got about halfway there before stepping down to greet her.

"You look beautiful, Libby," he murmured.

"Thank you." She felt herself blush. "I love you."

"I love you too."

"Take care of my girl," Grandpa said, before kissing her cheek.

"Always." Shane solemnly shook her grandfather's hand, then drew her forward, helping her step up to the church altar. Shane's brother Chase stood beside him as the best man, and she'd asked Alexis to be her maid of honor.

And as the pastor began their wedding ceremony, she felt the strength of God's love shining down upon them.

I HOPE you enjoyed Libby and Shane's story. Are you ready to read about Alexis and Griff in *Scent of Death*? Click Here!

DEAR READER

Thanks for reading *Scent of Fear*! I hope you enjoyed Shane and Libby's story. I'm having so much fun writing about the Sullivan family. I hope you are enjoying them as much as I am. And please stay tuned for *Scent of Death*, which will be Alexis and Griff's story. You won't want to miss that one.

Don't forget, you can purchase ebooks or audiobooks directly from my website and will receive a 15% discount by using the code **LauraScott15**.

I adore hearing from my readers! I can be found through my website at https://www.laurascottbooks.com, via Facebook at https://www.facebook.com/LauraScottBooks, Instagram at https://www.instagram.com/laurascottbooks/, and Twitter https://twitter.com/laurascottbooks. Please take a moment to subscribe to my YouTube channel at youtube.com/@LauraScottBooks-wr1xl?sub_confirmation=1. Also take a moment to sign up for my monthly newsletter to learn about my new book releases! All subscribers receive a free novella not available for purchase on any platform.

Until next time,

Laura Scott

PS. Keep reading for a sneak peek of *Scent of Death* . . .

SCENT OF DEATH

Chapter One

Alexis Sullivan kept pace with her K9, a black and white border collie named Denali, as they moved through a section of the Bighorn Mountains. This search area was new for them, a slight deviation from where her older sister Jessica and her now-husband, Logan, had found the piece of tail fin they believed came from their parents' plane crash.

"Search napoo!" she called encouragingly. Not that Denali showed signs of slowing down. Her K9 loved to work despite their mission being to find human remains. The term *napoo* basically meant finished, done, dead. And all cadaver handlers used the term rather than telling their dog to search for dead bodies.

Despite the grim task, Alexis had purposefully chosen this area of expertise to help during natural disasters. She and Denali had worked wildfire sites in California to tornado wrecks in North Carolina. The fact that her parents had never been found after their small plane had crashed over five years ago now had also factored into her decision. Which was why she was here in the mountains working with her K9.

Denali swept her keen nose over the ground as they walked. Alexis was working alone today, as summer was the busiest time for the Sullivan K9 Search and Rescue Ranch. Everyone else was out and about, doing things. She was the middle child of nine siblings, all of whom worked with dogs in various specialties. Denali was the only cadaver dog on the ranch, though, so this specific task wasn't something the other K9s could help with.

The sound of a dead tree branch snapping had her whirling around to scan the foliage behind her. Probably a large elk or a bear moving through the woods. She lightly touched the can of bear spray on her utility belt to reassure herself she was ready if needed.

She carried a firearm, too, and her oldest brother, Chase, made sure every one of the Sullivan siblings could shoot accurately. But a small handgun may not be enough to take down a bear, unless she was able to hit the animal in the heart or brain.

Not that she wanted to kill a bear or any other wild animal for that matter. She understood and accepted the hunting her brothers did, and she didn't even mind eating venison and elk meat, but the actual hunting part wasn't something she personally enjoyed.

Seeing nothing alarming, she rolled her shoulders beneath the heavy pack and tried to relax. Turning, she continued up the mountain. Denali was still working through the brush, her nose sniffing along the ground. Her dog was so good she'd picked up the scent of human ashes. Many cadaver K9s couldn't do that. Even so, sometimes Alexis wondered if searching for her parents' remains was a fruitless effort. What could possibly be left of them after five and a half years?

Yet she couldn't just give up either. Jessica finding the tail fin of the plane had spurred the siblings into renewing their search efforts. Especially since the piece of plane debris had been found a good fifty miles from their original search zone.

Why her parents' small plane had gone down was a mystery. Their youngest sibling, Kendra, kept insisting the crash was no accident. And while Alexis secretly agreed, the problem was that there was really no motive to kill them.

Well, there was the fact that her parents had been worth millions of dollars, something she and the other siblings hadn't known until after they'd been declared dead. The money was in a trust that covered the expenses of the ranch in addition to a modest salary for each of the siblings. Maya and Chase, the two eldest siblings, held family meetings every six months to go over the finances. Somehow, the trust continued to grow despite the often-difficult economic times. The money would have been a motive if not for the fact that her parents had everything buttoned up in the trust, and the only heirs were the nine kids.

And as far as she knew, nobody had tried to get the money from them. In fact, the Sullivan family had managed to keep the extent of their wealth a secret. Turning the former dude ranch into a search and rescue operation had been Maya's idea. Chase had eagerly agreed. They performed SAR services across the state of Wyoming, even venturing into Idaho, Montana, and Colorado. And the only payment they accepted were bags of dog food. They had nine K9s—well, ten now with the new puppy, Bear—to feed. One bag of dog food was basically a drop in the bucket of what they went through each week.

She gave Maya and Chase a lot of credit for holding the family together after her parents went missing. Their Christian faith had gotten them through the early dark days, and now many of her siblings were getting married and starting families.

Not that she was planning to head down that path. Especially not after two of her previous boyfriends had cheated on her.

Denali disappeared from her line of sight. Alexis quickened her pace, not wanting the K9 to get too far ahead. As she crested a ridge, she relaxed when she saw Denali sniffing near a bush.

"Break time," she called. K9s needed frequent breaks while working. They expended a lot of energy sniffing their surroundings, and with the hot July sun overhead, she needed to make sure her dog didn't become dehydrated.

Denali lifted her head and bounded toward her. Alexis glanced around, wishing she could get rid of the niggling warning sensation along the back of her neck. *Even if someone is out here*, she told herself, *there is nothing to worry about*. Stumbling across a fisherman or small-game hunter wouldn't be a threat. Alexis took a moment to find a shady spot near some trees and shrugged out of her pack.

In truth, she needed the break more than Denali. Taking her water bottle from the pack, she filled a collapsible bowl for her K9. As Denali lapped at the water, Alexis drained what was left in the bottle.

"Good girl," she praised as Denali stretched out on the ground. "You're doing a great job."

Denali's brown eyes gazed into hers. She leaned forward to hug the dog, then glanced at her watch. They'd been working for an hour, taking a meandering path, and she needed to make sure they could get back to the two-track road where she'd left her SUV.

"We'll go for one more hour, then turn back, okay?" She stroked Denali's soft fur. "I know you won't mind a long nap on our way back to the ranch."

Denali thumped her tail in agreement.

After fifteen minutes, she rose to her feet and offered Denali a little more water. Keeping a dog's mucus membranes moist was key during search and rescue missions. The moisture helped enhance the scent particles, and for cadaver dogs, that was even more important as the scents were often deeply buried in the ground.

"Search napoo!" She threw her arm wide. "Search!"

Denali eagerly went back to work, trotting along some invisible path that only her dog could smell. Alexis shouldered into her pack and quickly followed. She glanced over her shoulder frequently but didn't see anything alarming.

And Denali didn't growl or indicate she noticed anything either.

But Alexis was so preoccupied she didn't immediately notice when Denali made an abrupt turn, heading toward a meadow to the east. She nearly tripped over a rock to keep up.

Denali had her nose down and was moving faster now, an indication she may have found something. Her parents? Alexis was afraid to hope.

"Search napoo," she said encouragingly. But she needn't have worried. Denali headed to an area, sniffed for long minutes, then sat and let out a sharp bark.

Her alert! Alexis couldn't see much but quickened her pace all the same. Then she abruptly slowed when she realized what Denali had found.

A hand. A badly bloated human hand that had clearly been nibbled on by local wildlife.

Her stomach twisted painfully as she approached. "Here, Denali," she called. Then she pulled the pink piggy from her backpack. "Good girl! Good girl, Denali!" She tossed the piggy into the air, then cautiously approached the gruesome hand.

Definitely female, she thought as she crouched near the spot where it was poking out from the earth. Denali hadn't found her parents' remains as she'd hoped. Based on her experience in other disaster missions, she knew this hand hadn't been there for long. A week or two at the most.

She didn't want to disturb what might have been a crime scene. Yet she needed to understand if the hand had been left there by some animal, or if it was connected to the rest of the body.

Edging as close as she dared, she stared at the bloated hand. That's when she noticed there was a tattoo of flowers encircling the wrist. That made her lean toward the possibility the hand belonged to a woman.

She took a step back, surveying the area. The area of the earth appeared to have been recently disturbed, but that wasn't conclusive evidence that the rest of the body was buried there. For all she knew, the body had been lying on top of the soil and got dragged away from the area, leaving just the hand behind.

With shaky fingers, she pulled her cell phone from the pack.

No service.

Stifling a sigh, she rummaged for the large, bulky satellite phone Chase had insisted they carry. There had been several cases over the past few months where one of the siblings had been stuck in the mountains without service.

The sat phones were nice but heavy. Within minutes, she heard ringing on the other end of the line.

"Sheriff's office, how may I direct your call?" a female voice asked.

"This is Alexis Sullivan, and my dog has found human remains near—"

A crack of gunfire had her stopping abruptly, ducking and running toward her K9.

She grabbed Denali's vest and pulled the dog into the shelter of the woods. She crouched behind some trees, her heart pounding as she realized she shouldn't have ignored the niggle of warning that had plagued her for the past mile.

The snapping branch had been from a human, not an animal as she'd assumed.

"Hello? Are you there?" the female voice asked from the sat phone.

"I'm here, but someone fired a gun at me. I need police backup!" Even as she said the words, she understood the fruitlessness of her request. Help was hours away at best.

She and Denali were on their own—with a gunman who could be the same person who'd buried the dead body.

"WHAT WAS THAT?" FBI Agent Griffin Flannery touched the earpiece attached to his radio. He was just leaving Greybull, Wyoming, but had pulled off to the side of the road when the call came through. "Did I hear Alexis Sullivan calling in about finding human remains?"

"Yes, and it sounds like someone is firing a gun at her," the dispatcher replied. The radio dispatch channel was open to various law enforcement officials, including the game warden, local police, and those in federal law enforcement.

Like him. His gut churned with the thought of Alexis and Denali being in danger. "What's their location?"

"One moment, please." The dispatcher was silent for a moment, then said, "I can send the coordinates, Griff. Looks like she's calling from the southeast portion of the Bighorn Mountains."

"Please do." He quickly executed a U-turn, grateful that he wasn't at his office in Cheyenne when this call came through. "I'm on my way. Are you sending deputies as well?"

"Yes, Deputy Paul Holland has been dispatched to her location," the dispatcher confirmed. "But he's farther out than you are."

"Roger that." Griff didn't have red lights and sirens built into his personal vehicle, but he planted his foot on the gas, going as fast as he dared on the curvy, winding road. "If Alexis calls again, please patch her through to me."

"Right away." The radio connection ended, and Griff focused on navigating the highway. Even with pushing the speed limit, he knew he was a solid thirty to forty minutes away.

If he was a praying man like the Sullivan family, he'd pray for Alexis to be safe. But he and God weren't on speaking terms since losing his young wife to cancer two years ago. All the prayers in the world hadn't helped save Grace's life.

With a frown, he focused on the brief conversation he'd overheard. Was the body Alexis had found related to the three missing girls he'd been investigating? They had no indication of foul play, but three missing teenagers had been enough to raise suspicions related to sex trafficking. He was tasked with coordinating a statewide response to the missing teenagers, as they were from different areas of the state. Most recently, a nineteen-year-old by the name of Wendy Evers had been reported missing. He'd been at a small home on the easternmost side of Greybull to interview the nineteen-year-old's grandmother Barbara Evers who claimed her granddaughter wouldn't pick up and leave without telling her.

Griff was inclined to believe her.

His radio crackled in his ear. "Griff?"

"Alexis?" He was relieved to hear her voice. "Are you okay?"

"We're fine, but I don't know exactly where the shooter is located." She spoke in a hushed voice, as if she didn't want anyone to overhear. "I had a weird feeling earlier in the search and heard a branch snapping, but I didn't see anything unusual. Well, until now."

"I'm on my way and so is Deputy Paul Holland." He wished he could fly to her side, but calling Logan or one of the other local pilots for a ride would take too long. Hopefully, he'd be at her side very soon. "Can you find a place to hide?"

"Yeah, but I don't want to get too far from the site where Denali found the human remains." She heard her murmur reassurances to Denali. "You need to see this, Griff. It looks to me like a recent death. Like within the past week or so."

"What exactly did Denali find?" His goal was to keep her talking. Listening to her voice was reassuring, as if nothing could happen as long as they were on the phone together. And he'd seen her K9, Denali, in action just a few weeks ago. All of the Sullivan K9 teams were impressive when it came to search and rescue missions.

"Just a hand so far. I can't tell you if the rest of the body is buried nearby or not. Unfortunately, the gunman has me pinned down." She sounded frustrated and worried at the same time. "I found some thick foliage, which is helping."

He would have given anything to be there with her right now. He wanted to ask why she was out there alone in the first place but decided against starting an argument. It was a beautiful, warm summer day; no reason Alexis couldn't hike in the mountains with her dog.

Except when that dog happened to find human remains and some idiot decided to fire a gun at her.

Griff managed to reach the location of Alexis's SUV quickly enough. There was no sign of Holland's sheriff's deputy vehicle, but that was too bad. No way was he waiting around while Alexis hid in the woods from a possible murderer.

Hiking to Alexis's specific location would be the longest part of the trip. He used his compass to double-check his coordinates, then headed into the woods, moving at a light jog. He'd been a runner before he'd had knee surgery and knew he could cover more ground this way. As long as he ignored the pain.

"Alexis? Can you hear me?" He used his radio to connect to her satellite phone.

"Yes, I'm here. Where are you?" Her voice sounded louder now. "I haven't heard anything for a while, so I think the shooter might be gone."

"Don't take any chances," he warned. "Stay where you are. I'll come to you, okay?"

"Of course, I'll be careful. I would never risk anything happening to Denali." She sounded weary. "But I can't help but wonder if the gunman is related to the hand we found."

He had a bad feeling that was exactly what was going on. "Listen, Alexis, I'm investigating three missing teenage girls. If that guy is connected to that, you need to stay far away."

There was a long moment of silence as she digested that bit of news. "How is it that nobody from the ranch has been called out to search for these girls?"

It was a good question. Griff had learned over the past two years that the Sullivans were often called for missing residents even before law enforcement. Not because the locals were wary of the police, but because the Sullivan family had a stellar reputation. Their skilled K9s had been used to solve many crimes.

He'd participated in several of them recently. He'd been so impressed he'd put in a request to have a K9 of his own. A request that had been promptly denied.

"I'll give you more information on them later," he promised. "I happened to be in Greybull following up on the most recent missing girl when your call came through."

"I'm glad you were so close," Alexis said. "I'll be here waiting."

"See you soon." He reluctantly ended the call. He quickened his pace, determined to reach her side sooner rather than later.

If he were honest, he'd admit to having a soft spot for Alexis Sullivan. Not just because she was pretty and smart, although she was both of those things. Compassionate too. No, he was more impressed with her dedication to the Sullivan search and rescue mission.

She was too young for him, though, almost seven years his junior. And even if she wasn't too young, too sweet, and too good for him, he wasn't interested in opening his heart to love. Not after losing his wife, Grace. He told himself he cared about Alexis and the other Sullivans as friends. They were good people, icons in the community.

Yet he couldn't deny that he'd be devastated if anything happened to Alexis or her dog.

As he ran, he kept a sharp eye out for anything suspicious. He wasn't an expert tracker like Chase Sullivan, but when he passed a spot where what appeared to be a freshly broken branch was lying in the ground, he paused and glanced around. Was this what Alexis had heard? Had the gunman been in this location? Looking up, he noticed the branch had been low enough that it could have been broken by a tall man.

Or someone wielding a rifle.

Telling himself not to be ridiculous, as there were tons of fallen branches lying on the ground, he pushed forward. Yet he'd noticed that most of the other debris on the ground appeared to have been weathered by the elements—the sun, wind, and rain.

Concern for Alexis had him pushing his injured knee to the limit. After what seemed like forever, but was only twenty minutes or so, he checked his coordinates.

He was getting close. Running through the woods had shortened the time it had taken for him to reach Alexis's location. He continued pushing forward, and it was another ten minutes later when he heard a voice call out, "Griff? Is that you?"

"Yes, it's me." He belatedly realized she'd been worried he was the gunman. "I'm roughly sixty yards away."

"I see you," she said. "Denali alerted me that someone was coming."

Thank goodness for her K9, he thought. He knew the border collie wasn't an attack dog the way her brother Shane's German shepherd, Bryce, was. But he had no doubt the dog would protect her against a threat.

Human or otherwise.

He caught a glimpse of Denali's black and white coat first, then Alexis herself emerged from the trees. He waved at her to stay back, then raised his voice. "FBI! Come out with your hands where I can see them!"

Silence.

Griff hadn't really anticipated the guy would cooperate in turning himself in but tried again. "This is Agent Flannery with the FBI! Come out with your hands resting on your head where I can see them!"

More silence. He wanted to believe that meant the guy was long gone, but he wasn't willing to bank his life or Alexis's on that. Still, sometimes alerting the bad guys that he was a federal agent was enough to make them leave.

After another long five minutes, he crossed the open meadow to the spot where Alexis and Denali waited in the trees. Thankfully, nobody opened fire on him.

"Hey, Griff." Alexis offered a weak smile. "Fancy meeting you out here."

It surprised him how much he wanted to haul her into his arms. He settled for a grin. "Glad to be of service." Then he sobered. "Where's the human hand you found?"

"This way." Alexis turned and led the way to the other side of the meadow. It took her a few minutes to pinpoint the area, but then she gestured. "It's over there. I tried not to get too close so I wouldn't disturb what could possibly be a crime scene."

"I appreciate that." He glanced over his shoulder, wondering how long it would take for Deputy Paul Holland to get there. Then he carefully approached the clearing. The hand was difficult to see at first because it was bloated, discolored, small, and lying on the ground.

But as he crept closer, more details became clear. He narrowed his gaze on the splayed fingers. A woman's hand? When he noticed the flowery vine tattoo encircling the wrist, he immediately knew the victim's name.

Not Wendy Evers, as he'd anticipated, but the second missing girl, eighteen-year-old Josie Allen. She'd been reported missing by her place of employment four weeks ago. Josie didn't have any family; she'd moved here from California a year ago, according to the Wooden Hammer bar where she worked.

And Josie had a tattoo just like that in the last photo he had of the young woman. But what didn't make any sense was that Josie went missing from Casper, Wyoming. A city that was a solid four-and-a-half- to five-hour drive from this remote location.

Not good. He'd never imagined that he'd find the remains of Josie Allen here in the Bighorn Mountains.

"What do you think?" Alexis asked. "Are the rest of the remains buried there?"

"Yeah, I believe so." He sat back on his heels, looking at the loosely packed ground. He was going to need more than one sheriff's deputy to help him. He'd need a team, including crime scene techs.

But worse than that, Griff grimly realized they weren't dealing with a human-trafficking ring, the way he'd originally thought.

This appeared to be the work of a serial killer.